Scoop

NAT LOGAN

Table of Contents

Acknowledgements

Scoop's story wouldn't be possible without a huge amount of people. Let's start off with Jessica Downing asking me if I'd ever write an inexperienced MMC over the age of 23. I'd just released War and was writing Bear's book. I had Scoop's cover and all I knew about him at that time, is he was an ex-cop and tech guy for the MC. Jessica's comment sparked the question *what if Scoop was a 35-year-old virgin and asked the woman he couldn't get out of his mind to help him learn*? I couldn't do this without all of you.

My PA and alpha reader Beth, thank you for pulling me out of the hole I wrote myself into. Kat, for agreeing to help me grow the Bluff Creek Brotherhood MC through sharing about it and having such fantastic ideas. Thank you to Gabi for beta reading for me.

Names are my kryptonite and when I came asking for them, all of you came running. All of you readers, who suggested names who fit the characters I was dreaming of, thank you!!! Leslee Sears Nevill for Bootstrap, Cruise and Salty. Trish Howard Sikes for Dodge. Kat Smitheram for Blue. My hubby and Kat Smitheram for Butcher. Gabi Brockelsby for Cowboy. Rose Ielg for Rose. Natasha Tucker for Natasha. If you have any questions after reading the book, come find me in my reader group on FB Steamy Swoony Romance Reads and we can chat.

Now, grab a drink and settle back. The Bluff Creek Brotherhood MC and the world of the women of Franks and Daughters Bail Bonds are ready to take you on a ride.

Bluff Creek Brotherhood MC, Original Chapter

President: Warrick "War" Shields

Vice President: Benton "Bear" Carter

Sgt at Arms: Cannon

Enforcer: Open

Road Captain: Speedy

Club Secretary/Tech: Derek "Scoop" Layton

Medic: Flick

Chaplain: Noah "Locks" Franks

Treasurer: deceased, Regina and Baron are covering.

Originals: Rascal (father to Bear), Baron (father to War, Roam, Gage)

Members: Roam, Cruise, Slice

Nomad: Compass

Ol' Ladies: Regina Shields, Remington Shields, Winchester Carter

Badass, Fierce Women unclaimed: Sarah Franks, Jesse Franks, Beth Franks, Kennedy (Bear's half-sister), Ellie (Beth and Winnie offered her a job in Bear's book.)

Bluff Creek Brotherhood MC, Cider Creek, Texas Chapter

President: Bootstrap

Vice President: Gage Shields

Sgt at Arms: Open

Enforcer: Salty

Road Captain: Dodge

Club Secretary: Blue

Medic: Butcher

Club Treasurer: Donner

Tech: Cowboy

Chaplain: Open

FRANKS AND *Daughters* BAIL BONDS

<u>CODES</u>

Code Monica: Everything's perfect. No injuries.

Code Ross: Everything's not okay. Help needed.

Code Janice: Going radio silent.

Code Rachel: Emotional backup needed. No questions asked.

Code Phoebe: Be ready with backup. Something's off but nothing pinpointed.

Code Chandler: Friendlies incoming.

Code Joey: Targets neutralized. Medical attention may be needed.

Code Burke: The old guys or originals have it.

Code Pancakes: The sisters lost their mom before the new codes were used. Pancakes was Kathryn's code for solving any problem. They'd meet around the table with pancakes and bacon and work through any problems. It stuck.

Code Marcel: Something's lost.

Code Balcony: Need some space.

Code Paulo: Can't trust the situation or person.

Prologue- Last Night

Scoop kept an eye on the woman he'd been falling for. Straight up head over heels, he couldn't imagine ever being happy without her. Add in the fact that no matter what woman was around or how skimpily she was dressed, he didn't get hard. Nope, his dick only perked up when she was around. And man, when she leaned over him to point out something on the computer, her hair falling across his shoulder smelling of vanilla, the fucker turned hard as steel. And if she had her blonde hair up in a messy bun on top of her head and her computer glasses on, his dick thought it was time to play ravish the hot librarian or hot tech nerd.

Too bad there were two things wrong with that scenario. First, he was positive he was in her friend zone. Being friends with the woman he couldn't get off his mind was a great start, but it wasn't where he wanted to stay. And second, he had zero experience ravishing a woman. A thirty-five-year-old virgin who hadn't even had a blow job. He didn't have any special reason. When he would have been going out in high school and later college, he was helping to raise his younger twin sisters and working two part-time jobs to put food on their table. His mom had struggled after his dad had left them. She'd worked a job while attending school to become a nurse. Scoop had done what he could to help them survive. There wasn't any time or funds for extras like dating. Then he was focused on getting into the police academy. Once he finally had some time to himself, he hadn't connected with anyone. If he'd waited that long to finally take care of his pesky virginity, he didn't want to just bang one out in a bar bathroom, though if she gave him the time of day, he'd do it anywhere.

To be that close to her, expose each delicious inch of her creamy skin and taste her would be his dream. Too bad he had no idea what to do. He'd never even asked a woman out.

Cannon was across the room talking to her. Scoop had never wanted to hit one of his friends more than when she laughed at something he said, tucking her hair behind her ear. Scoop was positive Cannon wasn't interested in her, but he envied the easy way Cannon flirted.

She was the whole package with brains, an hourglass figure he wanted to explore, and a personality that had him craving her presence.

Flick tapped him on the shoulder. "When are you going to make your move?"

Scoop shook his head, tossed back another drink. He wasn't sure what number drink it was, but everything was getting nice and fuzzy. Fuzzy helped because then it didn't hurt so much if she ignored him. "She thinks I'm a friend. She doesn't see me like that."

Flick sipped his beer, then tilted the bottle toward her. "Then build on that. Friends, then friends with benefits. You could ask her to help you with a favor. Getting rid of a certain status you have. Then, when she falls for all the deliciousness of Mint Chocolate Chip, slip a ring on her finger and walk her down the aisle before she comes out of the sex daze."

Flick was a prankster, and Scoop wasn't sure if he was serious or not. He might like her calling him that name but no one else was allowed. He was fine with the name Scoop.

They wouldn't be changing it to any of the ice cream flavors she called him.

"Are you joking or really suggesting I should do that?" Sober, he had a hard time knowing if Flick was joking. He was well past happy drunk and moving into not feeling any pain drunk. Flick was going to have to be a little clearer for Scoop to understand.

Flick laid his hand on Scoop's shoulder. "Man, you've been falling for her since the first time you all collaborated on tech stuff. Think about this: Do you want to be her friend and then maybe watch someone else romance her, or do you want to go after the woman who puts a look on your face I've never seen there before?"

He nodded, then swallowed. His mouth was dry despite the amount of liquor he'd consumed, and his heart pounded loud enough that his chest felt like he was near the speakers at a rock concert. He licked his lips, then decided to hell with it. The worst that could happen is she'd say no. He grabbed another drink and downed it. A little liquid courage was needed for this. He weaved over to where Sarah was standing in her dress from the wedding. It highlighted her breasts with her cleavage on display. He imagined diving in and pleasing her any way he could. Cannon had walked away from Sarah which was good because he'd hate having to do this in front of his friend.

"Could I talk to you about something?" He worked to keep his words from slurring. The lights they'd hung to give Remington her dream wedding lit Sarah's hair like a halo. She was so beautiful.

Sarah didn't answer right away, gazing into his eyes. She must have found the answer she needed because she nodded.

She headed to the side of the yard, closer to the orchard entrance. He followed behind her, trying to enjoy the sight of her rounded bubble butt cupped by her bridesmaid's dress, but he was focusing on not throwing up. What if he ruined everything? What if she laughed at him? He wasn't sure he could handle her ridicule.

She paused at the entrance to the orchard. "What do you need?"

What did he need? He needed to cup her face in his hands, lay his lips against her and claim her. He wanted to see if she tasted as good as she smelled.

"I need to know if you'd be willing to help me with something."

Sarah smiled at him. Why did his heart feel better when she smiled? They could be frustrated and searching for a thread of information. She'd smile, and bam! Everything was better.

"Sure, if I can. Whatcha need, Rocky Road?"

"It's a huge favor, and I honestly don't know what to say." His skin felt too tight, and he was sweating. Hopefully, she couldn't see it on his forehead.

"How about you just ask?"

Ask. He could do that, but he couldn't wait another minute. He stepped closer, sliding his arm around her waist. Man, she smelled good. The sweet smell of cookies and banana bread. The smell that made him hungry to gorge himself on sweets. It's what he wanted to do with Sarah. Gorge himself until he was satisfied. Her soft, full breasts pressed against his chest.

"I see you as a friend I can trust, and I have a situation I need help with. Will you trust me to try something?"

Her eyes pulled him in. He could happily fall into them and gaze into their pale blue-green depths forever. She nodded. He slid his fingers into her blonde, silky hair, grasping the back of her head. His lips touched hers, tasting vanilla from the cake he'd watched her eat earlier. The taste and feel of finally having her in his arms had him hardening enough to pound nails. She squirmed against him, rubbing against his zipper. If only he had the right to take her back to his room and unwrap her from her dress. Her lips were everything he'd imagined, and he wanted to continue kissing her, but he had a question.

He pulled away, gazing Into her eyes, breathing a little heavier. "You said we're friends, and we obviously have chemistry."

"Yes, but..."

His finger stilled her words, rubbing along her top lip. Her soft lips against his finger had him wondering if she was this soft all over. Her face blurred a little. Maybe he'd had little more than he should, but he'd craved this for so long. He wasn't stopping now.

"I never really planned on having to ask someone this, but I'm still inexperienced. I heard you and your sisters talking so I know you're not. Will you teach me about sex?"

His alcohol-soaked brain catalogued her eyes filling with heat. He hoped that meant she was going to say yes. He wasn't sure how he'd survive if she said no.

He trailed his fingers down her cheek, the smooth skin of her neck calling his name. Her neck wavered and then there were two of her necks. Hmmm, double his pleasure.

"Scoop, are you okay?" Sarah's voice came from far away. His vision darkened, and he reached for Sarah. He needed something from her. What had they been talking about?

Oh man, his stomach was roiling. He pulled away from Sarah. What had they been talking about? He realized he wasn't going to stop his stomach. He moved away from Sarah, turning to the side and bending at the waist as all the alcohol and food made a reappearance. The smell it made as it splashed onto the ground and up onto his pants and shoes had him vomiting some more.

Then everything started to darken. Oh fuck.

SARAH WATCHED AS SCOOP lurched to the side and started vomiting all over. It splashed up onto him, onto her sandals and all over her pretty, polished toenails. He'd obviously consumed vast amounts of alcohol because the smell was overwhelming and ripe. Vomit didn't usually bother her, but the only thing keeping her from puking beside him was her worry for him. She yelled for help as Scoop's eyes closed and he began to crumple to the ground. She grabbed his arm to make sure he didn't hit his head against the fence on the way down and also so he wouldn't land in the vomit. The smell was horrendous, and she didn't want anyone to have to deal with getting him clean. Flick dropped down beside her, rolling Scoop to his back.

"What happened?" Flick asked as he checked Scoop's pulse.

"He was talking to me, then started weaving back and forth. He bent over and vomited, then his eyes closed, and he hit the ground. I could smell liquor on his breath. Do you think he's that drunk?"

Flick opened Scoop's eyes and shone a light in them. Flick always seemed to be prepared to take care of them. He had a pen with a light on the end he always carried.

"I was hanging out with him before he walked over to you. He'd had some drinks and then pounded a couple." Flick motioned to the pile of vomit. "He probably just got a lot of it out of his system. I'll get Cannon and we'll get him cleaned up a little and to his room. I'll keep an eye on him tonight."

Sarah nodded as Cannon and Flick lifted Scoop by his arms and legs, carrying him into the clubhouse. Despite Cannon and Flick's size, Scoop wasn't a lightweight. He wasn't your typical computer nerd. Yeah, he had the adorable glasses, but he worked out with the guys. His arms were well-developed, and she'd watched how much he could bench press when they were in the gym together. Cannon and Flick seemed to have zero problem carrying him, despite his size. She ran ahead and opened the door. Flick nodded his thanks.

"What are we doing with him?" Cannon asked.

"You're going to help me get him in the shower and rinsed off. We'll toss his clothes in the washer, get him settled in bed with a bucket by him, and I'll check him periodically."

Cannon nodded, smiling at Sarah as she opened the door to Scoop's room. "We've got this." Cannon's tone didn't allow for any questioning of his words. Flick closed Scoop's door once they got past it.

Sarah stood in the hallway. What the ever-lovin' fuck had just happened? Scoop had slid his arms around her, laid his lips against hers, and given her the best kiss ever. She read how women in romance novels were swept away by a kiss, but today, she'd experienced it. With one kiss, he'd shown her everything she'd been missing. A kiss had never had her nipples harden and her panties dampen. She'd wanted to slide her hand up into his hair and see if it was as soft as she'd imagined. And she'd imagined a lot, late at night, in her bed.

Then he'd blown her mind when he'd said he was a virgin. A thirty-five-year-old virgin who wanted to have her teach him about sex. Yeah, she had some experience. She hadn't gotten to be forty-one years old without having a couple of relationships that had progressed to the sex stage, but she wasn't someone with tons of experience.

She and Scoop were phenomenal friends, great co-workers when needed and sure, she'd dreamed of having them be more. Between his tousled brown hair that she constantly wanted to run her hands through and his glasses, which he continually pushed into place on his nose, she frequently had to remind herself *they were friends*.

Despite the alcohol coursing through his system, he'd still blushed when he'd asked her to teach him. His blush was one of the things she loved, no, liked about him. She didn't love him. That wasn't their relationship.

She wrinkled her nose when she realized the smell of vomit wasn't just on Scoop. She could smell it on herself. She glanced down and realized her sandals had chunks clinging to them. Blech. Now that she knew Flick had Scoop under control, her stomach turned at the smell. She headed outside. She'd use the hose by the garden to get the worst of it off before she headed home, or she'd be tossing her cookies on the ground too, and she despised throwing up.

She walked outside and over to the garden hose. She turned it on and let the water rinse across her shoes. The cold water was a shock after the heat of Scoop's kiss, but maybe it would cool her down. She finished rinsing her feet and shoes, then checked before walking toward her car. She didn't want to deal with anyone right now.

She had a lot to do in the next two weeks and she didn't have time to consider Scoop's offer, request, or whatever she could call it tonight. Her plans for the on-site daycare were going ahead. To ensure it was a safe place and no one besides family knew the safety features, they were closing the offices while the changes were made.

They'd instituted a mandatory two-week vacation for all employees in Bluff Creek, and Sarah couldn't wait. She'd never had two weeks off and she was taking full advantage of it. She'd already scoped out where she wanted to visit. She wasn't staying in her house for two weeks, though she'd usually be perfectly happy reading, sewing, and baking for two weeks, but she craved an adventure. There were places she wanted to see, things she wanted to shop for, and items to check off her bucket list. Now if she could keep her sisters from horning in, that would be great. She adored her sisters, but she wanted a break to be just Sarah Franks. Not Sarah Franks, computer guru or Sarah Franks, second oldest sister or Locks' daughter, a princess of the Bluff Creek Brotherhood MC. She was going to do what she liked, when she liked, and no one was going to be in charge of her, including going to a book signing while she was off. There was no way she was letting her sisters know about that. They all loved reading and heck, Remington would leave her newly wedded husband in a second if she thought she could meet some of her favorite authors.

She was also going to hit up some flea markets for some of the retired Fiestaware she collected. She'd been wanting a vase in a hard-to-find color and maybe a couple serving pieces. Her mom had collected it over the years. It had been their everyday dishes, but her dad had bought her mom a specialty piece every anniversary. Their table was always colorful and festive. When her mom had passed, she and her sisters had split the pieces. Her dad said he didn't need it and they should all enjoy it. Splitting between the five sisters meant to have a good collection, she had to do some searching.

Maybe by the time she got back from her trip, she would have forgotten about the possibility of teaching Rocky Road about sex. What would it be like to show a man exactly what you liked and how you liked it? To try all those positions talked about in her books and see if they really did make her forget her own name. Having sex on a motorcycle was one of the things she'd always wondered about. How did you balance and move without ending up calling 911? Nah, she shouldn't even have those thoughts in her head. They were friends and co-workers. What if she screwed it all up? Scoop was the first person she actually enjoyed working with. Sure, her team was fine, but sometimes, when she had to explain the same concept for the fifth time, she got a tad annoyed. But she had to wonder. Did the blush on his face and neck appear on his chest? Did he have tattoos on his chest? Was he smooth or hairy? Too many questions and she really shouldn't be considering what he said.

There were too many possibilities of her screwing up their relationship, but a small part of her wondered, what if it didn't?

Chapter One

Scoop held still as he catalogued how he felt. His throat was scratchy and sore. His head pounded with the beat of his heart and his stomach ached. He cautiously opened his eyes. Faint sunlight had him squinting in pain at the glare. He turned toward his side table, wrinkling his nose at the rank smell in the room.

He wasn't sure if he was the source of the smell or if it was the bucket he clocked beside the bed. A glass of water and a bottle of pain reliever were on his bedside table along with a note propped against it. He laid the note down until he twisted open the bottle and dropped two pain relievers in his hand. He thought better of it and added another two. He needed something to beat this headache. He tossed the tablets in his mouth and gulped the water until it was gone.

He was so thirsty. He concentrated on getting out of bed, tying off the bag in the trash can to empty it, then headed to his en suite bathroom. He emptied his bladder, surprised he had anything to piss. He brushed his teeth because he couldn't stand the fuzzy feel to his teeth and tongue while turning on the shower to heat up. A sniff of his armpits let him know the trash can wasn't the only thing that was rancid in the room.

He stepped into the shower, relishing the feel of the hot water while ignoring thinking about last night and his colossal screw up. He tried to keep his mind off Sarah, but washing his cock had him wishing she was the one taking care of him. He pushed those thoughts out of his mind.

Although Sarah seemed the sweetest of the sisters, he didn't see any way he was coming back from his pukefest in front of her. Nope, he'd blown every chance he had. Time to face the music because he knew his brothers wouldn't let him live his fiasco down. They'd always have his back but had no problem razzing him while doing it.

He dried off, tossing his towel in the basket and wiped down the counter, then dressed before looking for his glasses. He picked them up from the bedside table, sliding them on. Time to face the music and see what the note said. He hoped and prayed it wasn't from Sarah saying she never wanted to see him again.

Drink some water, take the pills, shower the stink off, and get your butt out to the front room. We're all taking a ride. We'll stop for breakfast and figure out how to help you recover from puke-a-palooza. That was Cannon's suggestion. I thought pukefest or puke festival, but everyone sided with Cannon. I still think mine were better.

Your friend who showered you and cleaned the puke off your face,

Flick

P.S. You might owe Sarah a new pair of sandals.

SCOOP GUIDED HIS BIKE over beside Flick's, turning to back it into the spot. Rascal, Locks, Cannon, and Baron had been waiting on him and hadn't said much before they got on their bikes.

He had to admit the thirty-minute ride had given him time to think and begin to feel human. They'd traveled all the way through the countryside before heading back toward town. They were meeting Bear at Regina's Roadside Refuge, and Scoop thought he could actually eat now without being nauseous.

He was a little worried about what Locks was going to say. He hoped Locks only knew he wanted to date Sarah and not that he'd asked her to teach him about sex. He'd be mortified, but he'd get through it.

Flick waited for him, and he appreciated it. He was letting the originals and Cannon get a little ahead of him. It was cowardly, but he was man enough to admit that. He had that same feeling in the pit of his stomach he used to feel when he was called to the principal's office. It had only happened a couple of times, but both times, he'd been petrified he was going to be suspended. He hadn't minded getting in trouble for what he'd done. He'd punched guys who didn't know to keep their hands to themselves when a girl said no. He'd only worried it would keep him from getting into the college and then the police academy. Both times, his principal had said he admired what Scoop had done but to not take chances like that. He should tell a teacher instead.

If the teacher in the hall had been doing his job, Scoop wouldn't have needed to get involved, but he'd kept that to himself. He hoped this get-together turned out as good as his visit to the principal office, but he'd have to get off his bike to go see.

Flick's hand gave a reassuring squeeze to his shoulder. "C'mon man. Time to face the music."

Scoop nodded and got off the bike and walked through the door.

Bear had seated them in the area they'd come to know as theirs. No matter how busy it got, he only sat those considered family to the MC at this table. Otherwise, if it wasn't Franks & Daughters Bail Bonds, the security company or Whiskey's family, the table sat unoccupied with a reserved sign on it. Although it could easily seat twelve people, they were all congregated toward one end. Flick sat down by Cannon, leaving one seat on Cannon's other side, but Locks motioned to the seat directly across from him. When Scoop didn't immediately walk toward it, Locks cocked his eyebrow, daring him to ignore the unspoken directive.

Scoop walked two steps forward, pulled the chair out and sat down, breathing deep, hoping this wasn't one of those 'keep away from my daughter' speeches. Locks still held the Chaplain position in the club and was one of the original members, but if Locks tried to tell him that he couldn't see Sarah, they'd have a problem.

Scoop fiddled with the napkin wrapped around his silverware, concentrating on unwrapping it. A plate of bacon, scrambled eggs, biscuits and gravy was slid in front of him as plates were placed in front of the others. He ate here enough that Bear didn't need to ask his order. Bear slid into the seat at the end of the table that had been open.

"Okay, so I only agreed you could all eat here after the ride if you didn't break anything or cause any issues with customers. No blood, no broken bones, and no broken furniture."

Cannon huffed, "I think taking the VP job has made you soft, brother."

"I'm not soft. I worked darned hard on getting this place perfect and someone's hurt feelings are not cause for it to be destroyed."

"Calm down, Bear. Nothing is going to get destroyed. If Scoop will look at me, we can discuss this as adults."

Scoop raised his head from his food, placing his fork on his plate and wiping his mouth with his napkin, trying not to let his fear show in his eyes.

"I've been reminded lately, rather loudly by Winnie, that I raised strong women who know their own mind. I don't need to give you permission to date Sarah, but what I will do is give you my blessing. My girl lights up when she's with you. Now, screw it up and you'll be sorry."

"Are you kidding me? Screw it up and you'll be sorry? Those are weak words," Cannon grumbled.

"Hey, I have a granddaughter that seems to have some type of radar when I say cuss words. I had to pay money the other day for calling the salesman an ass after he left and I'd like to have..."

"Papa Locks, you owe the swear jar," Phoebe's young voice rang out.

Locks turned around and looked toward the doorway, smiling at her. "Phoebe, what are you doing here?"

Scoop guessed she'd been hanging out with her Aunt Jesse. Phoebe had on pink coveralls almost identical to what Jesse wore in the garage. Phoebe's had HCIC stitched on the pocket.

"Aunt Jesse and Aunt Beth are teachin' me. I learned bout buretors. Now we're getting fuel for our bodies. Then Aunt Beth said it's time for disgustus." Phoebe slid under Locks' arm, settling herself on his lap, and held out her hand.

"How about you give me a pass this time? I don't want to take time away from your disguise training." Locks picked up a piece of bacon to tempt Phoebe.

"Hold on, Papa. I gots an idea the aunties helped me with." Phoebe turned her head and yelled, "Aunties!" right in Flick's ear. Flick jerked at the sound but smiled at Phoebe. She was so darn cute and sweet they all doted on her.

Jesse walked in with Beth. Jesse paused, then took the seat by Baron, leaving the one by Cannon for Beth.

"What do you need, Phoebe?"

"Papa Locks doesn't want to pay me for the swear. What was I offerin' him?"

Jesse and Beth broke out in giggles. "Dad, Phoebe told us you all are in breach of the oral agreement you agreed to. She said you all keep trying to have her give you a pass." Beth glared at Locks.

"So, we suggested she and the kids offer you a subscription service. If you're on their service, then you're covered if you accidentally say a swear." Jesse's grin was mischievous. Scoop had to admit a subscription was brilliant. Phoebe and the kids would have their college or trade schools paid for before they were ten, knowing his MC brothers.

"Hmph, and how much is this subscription going to cost me?" Locks grumbled.

"The first ten people get a discount." Phoebe smiled and tilted her head at Locks, batting her lashes. Obviously, the sisters had been coaching Phoebe because he'd never seen her do that before, but he was more than happy to have the focus off him and on something else.

He was relieved Locks wasn't outright against him and Sarah dating, but he had some concerns trying to date Sarah with all the nosiness that came with his MC family.

He wanted more than sex from Sarah, but he wasn't sure she would be ready for that, so asking her to help him get some experience had seemed the perfect option. Whether his judgment had been compromised from too much alcohol was a moot point now. He'd asked her and he'd have to live with the consequences.

"What type of discount?" Rascal questioned.

"Fifty person."

"Fifty percent for six months," Beth corrected.

Locks shook his head. "What exactly is this subscription going to cost me?"

Phoebe looked at Beth, and Beth mouthed only forty dollars to her. Phoebe snuggled into Locks and put her little hand on his face. "Only forty dollars, Papa Locks."

Locks huffed a little and smiled. "So twenty bucks with the discount?"

"Yep. Jesse said that's a bargain.'"

"Count me in, Phoebe." Locks pulled out six twenties and handed them over. "Six months, and does this cover just you, Phoebe, or all the cousins? I mean, from your coveralls, you're the head cousin in charge, if I'm guessing right."

Phoebe glanced at Beth. "It covers all the cousins. They're splitting the income, but that doesn't mean you won't hear them get after you for swearing. You'll just know you don't have to pay anymore that month. And yes, since Phoebe's the oldest, she's the head cousin in charge," Beth explained.

"We considered some other ones, but Phoebe vetoed them." Jesse shook her head and smiled at Phoebe.

"Yep, I'm no friggin' princess. I'm a warrior." Phoebe accepted the bacon Locks had been offering her after he dropped his money on the table. She snuggled closer. "Thanks, Papa Locks."

Rascal handed Phoebe a buttered biscuit with some sandhill plum jelly. "Here you go, warrior."

Phoebe grinned at Rascal. "Thanks, Papa Rascal."

"I'm in."

"Me too."

"Yep, I want the discount."

The comments flew fast and furious because they'd all paid major bucks at a dollar a swear since Phoebe and the kids had come to live with Bear and Winnie. Beth pulled a notebook from her pocket and started a list indicating if they prepaid.

Locks glanced over at Scoop, "Don't think we're finished chatting, Scoop?"

"Are we discussing last night? What did Beth and I miss?"

"This is between Scoop and Locks, Jesse. You need to mind your own business," Cannon muttered.

"So, I guessed you missed that I'm Sarah's sister. You may be a brother in the MC, but it doesn't give you the right to tell me what to do." Even in pink overalls, Jesse's glare had him hoping she didn't turn her irritation to him.

"I was just telling Scoop I raised strong women, and he doesn't need my permission."

Scoop worked to keep from laughing because he noticed Locks didn't mention his blessing or his threat. Watching Locks' family interact made him miss his mom and sisters more than usual. His mom's contract with the traveling nurse job she had was up soon. Maybe he could convince her to try out Bluff Creek for a while. He hadn't wanted her and his sisters anywhere near his old job and the chief, with good reason.

Now, he'd love to have his sisters and mom visit or move here. It had grown quiet. He glanced over and Beth and Jesse were staring at him. How had he missed Rascal and Phoebe walking over by the sweets counter in the room?

"I'm so glad Dad said you don't need permission because Sarah is her own woman," Jesse said.

"However, as her sisters, we want you to know that you fuck it up, there won't be a hole big enough for you to hide in. Now, if you part friends after dating, no harm, no foul. You treat her like less than the wonderful woman she is and we'll use you for target practice. I rarely miss," Beth had lowered her voice, leaning closer across the table toward him.

"I heard you whisper, Aunt Beth. That's a swear, but you gots the sub'kiption so you're okay. Just don't make it a habit."

As the youngest, he'd wondered if Beth was the baby of the family and not as tough as her sisters. Seeing her laying down the law to him kind of scared him a little. She wasn't a pushover and was just as tough as her older sisters.

"Got it. I plan on working to date Sarah if she can forgive me after the whole puke on the shoes fiasco."

He endured his friends' laughter because he deserved it. If it hadn't happened to him, he would think it was hilarious. He'd deal with the puke considering the liquor gave him enough courage to kiss Sarah and that kiss had been everything he imagined and more. The feel of her soft lips against his and the taste when she'd allowed his tongue entrance had been perfection.

"She'll forgive you. I mean, it's not like you slept with her and then never mentioned it again, right?" Jesse patted his shoulder.

Beth and Jesse stood up, sliding their chairs back in. Beth grabbed two pieces of bacon off Locks' plate. "Later, Dad." Beth grabbed Phoebe's hand as Jesse carried their box of goodies out.

Locks waited until they left before shaking his head. "I love my daughters, but sometimes it's like a typhoon when they walk in the room. Where were we?"

Baron chuckled. "Give it up, Locks. You've lost the upper hand scaring him when you were worried about cussing and Phoebe catching you. Let's eat and Scoop can tell you about his family. I know your dad isn't around. What about your mom?"

Scoop sipped his coffee, relieved they were moving to other topics. Maybe he'd actually survive this.

"My mom is a nurse practitioner and finishing up her last assignment. She's been a traveling nurse for the last four years and has lived in her RV. I'm hoping she might come visit Bluff Creek."

He watched Locks and Baron have a whole conversation with only their eyes.

"Do you think she'd be interested in running her own clinic?" Baron questioned.

"I don't know. She has advanced training so she'd be qualified."

"Locks, Rascal, and I have been discussing that with everything happening, it would be nice to not rely on only

Flick. We chatted with War about it and he said to explore the possibilities and have it ready to be voted on when he gets back. If your mom would be interested, I think between the MC, the security company, and our other projects, we could pay her a good salary."

"I own the building across from the sheriff's office and I'd be more than happy to use it as a clinic if your mom wanted to run it. She could be on call for all of us but also offer services for people in town. It's a pain for the ones with kids to have to drive thirty miles to a doctor's office," Locks stated.

"Why don't you contact your mom and see if she'd even be interested? If she is, we can work up a proposal. Maybe a six-month contract to let her see if she likes it. We can vote on it when War gets back." Baron motioned for another refill of coffee while he waited on Scoop.

"I'll ask her. I've been meaning to check in with her."

He couldn't imagine his mom not loving Bluff Creek. She adored small towns, and her skills were needed. Two things his mom couldn't resist. Now, if he could figure out how he was going to approach Sarah. *Sorry I puked on you, but what did you think of my request* didn't really sound very romantic.

Chapter Two

S arah opened the oven door, leaning back so the steam and heat escaped. She tugged the rack out, holding it with her potholder. Grabbing a toothpick, she slid it into the biggest loaf of pumpkin bread. Seeing it come out clean, she grabbed the other potholder to lift out the loaf and place it on her cooling rack. She quickly removed the other eleven loaves. She'd done enough for everyone to have two, including her dad, who'd have to wait until tomorrow for his.

It had been five days since Scoop had made his unexpected proposal. In the course of that time, they'd usually see each other at least twice with how their jobs intersected, but not this week. No texts, no calls, and no email. He'd been silent. She wasn't sure if he was embarrassed or regretted asking her. After she'd spent time trying to figure out what to do, she'd given in and sent a Code Rachel today. Her sisters had all responded they'd make it.

She was worried she wasn't seeing things clearly, and between all of them, with all their different personalities, she'd get a good idea if she was on track or not. Her dad called it answer averaging. Ask at least three people the same thing, then compare their answers to what you'd thought.

The door slammed. "If I'm first here, I'm grabbing all the bread and running. That smells incredible and I don't want to share."

She giggled at her youngest sister's words. They all loved her pumpkin bread and fought over it, but she'd made plenty. Beth walked into the kitchen, laying a tray of her chocolate chip cookies on the island. Her sister made the best chocolate chip cookies and even though she'd tried, Beth's were still better.

"Trade you a cookie for a slice of pumpkin bread. Ooh, yum. You made honey butter too." Beth was already buttering a slice of pumpkin bread without waiting for her answer, but Sarah wasn't surprised. Being at her sisters' houses was like being at her own. They'd been close as sisters, but when their mom had died of cancer, they'd become closer.

She picked up one of Beth's cookies, taking a large bite, savoring the taste of vanilla, butter-flavored Crisco, and chocolate chips. "So good, Beth."

Remington, Jesse, and Winnie walked in, each carrying snacks to share. Joey was wrapped up in Winnie's arms. "Hope it's okay I brought Joey. Bear decided he and War should take the kids for a ride. I know Rascal or Dad would have fought over him, but I also knew you guys hardly ever get him to yourselves."

Sarah washed her hands and reached for him. "Gimme. You guys can grab snacks while I cuddle for a minute."

"Plus, let's face it. Spilling your guts is easier if you're holding a baby." Remington cocked her eyebrow at Sarah. Yes, it would be easier, but she had no doubt one of them would take Joey as soon as possible. The grandpas hogged Joey and his aunts had to fight to hold him.

Jesse settled on one of the chairs at the island, buttering her pumpkin bread. "So, I'm hazarding a guess this has something to do with a certain someone laying a super-hot kiss on you at Remi's wedding, then puking his guts out afterward."

"Wait, I missed that. What was I doing?" Remi questioned.

"Oh, it's when you and War snuck off and banged one out beside the barn," Jesse chuckled as Remi's face turned a dark burgundy.

"Umm, no we..."

Jesse shook her head, then in a perfect imitation of Remi's voice, replied, "Please, War, harder. I won't break." Then she switched to a deep voice reminiscent of War, "Oh, wife. I will. You'll feel me until next week."

Laughter filled the kitchen as Remi's blush deepened. "Whatever."

"You should thank me. I stopped at least two other couples from finding your hiding spot and had to listen to you all fuck."

"Thank you," Remi grudgingly answered. "Now, let's get to Scoop. Is that why we're here?"

Sarah took a sip of her iced tea. She should have pulled out the hard stuff but she hadn't found a liquor yet that tasted good with her pumpkin bread.

"So, Mint Chocolate Chip came over, asked me if I trusted him, then claimed my lips. It was just like everything we read in our books. His taste, his touch, his smell were perfect, and I didn't want him to stop. Then he pulled away and dropped his bombshell. He's a virgin and wants me to teach him about sex."

Remington, Jesse, and Winchester's eyes bugged out with surprise, but Beth just smiled and nodded. Her sisters stared at their youngest.

"You knew. How?" Winnie asked.

"I guessed. Even though all the girls flock to him, I've never seen him take someone back to his room or anywhere else for that matter, plus hello, my job is surveillance. I don't quit keeping an eye on things just because I'm not out on a job."

"So, what do you think about teaching him? He's super cute in a nerdy sort of way. The pushing the glasses up his nose, then running his fingers through his wavy brown hair is attractive." Jesse grabbed a cookie from underneath Remi's hand before she could get it.

Remi shook her head. "There are plenty of cookies. You didn't have to grab that one."

"There weren't plenty of cookies with the perfect number of chocolate chips." Jesse followed her words by sticking her tongue out, which was covered in chewed up cookie and chocolate chips.

"You are so juvenile." Remi rolled her eyes, then grabbed another cookie to eat.

"Ladies, and I use that term loosely, could we get back to Jesse's question? What are you going to do? I mean, whew, getting to teach the man you crushed on how to please you in bed. That is hot." Winnie fanned her face.

She'd known getting her sisters together was the best thing to do, having them gathered around her island waiting to help her with whatever she needed. They always had her back. None of them had brought up that she was forty-one and Scoop was thirty-five as a deterrent.

"I don't know. He's a really good friend, and I value his friendship, but what if this screws everything up? Say I do this, and I fall for him. What if he doesn't feel the same way, and I have to watch him fall in love with someone else?"

Remi's arm slipped around her shoulder. "Mom always told us life doesn't come with a guarantee. I want you to consider something. If you say no, will you regret it later?"

Beth pushed another cookie toward her, and she couldn't resist. Chocolate and brown sugar solved a lot of things but this time, she had to decide. Was it worth possibly changing their friendship to something more?

She chewed, listening to her sisters chat and fight over who got to hold Joey next. She enjoyed being around Scoop. They never ran out of things to talk about, and she did use him in her spank bank because he was the only man she pictured when she thought about sex. It all came down to: would she regret it if she said no? How would she feel a year down the road if she said no and she saw him with someone else? Could she live with it if she didn't at least try?

Chapter Three

S coop slid out from under his Bronco and wiped his hands on the cloth. His Bronco was coming along, but none of the new parts had come in. He was just trying to keep his hands and mind busy so he couldn't think about the complete clusterfuck he'd made of talking to Sarah. How did you come back from puking on someone? Cannon had been more than happy to share that little tidbit that he'd puked hard enough it had hit the ground with so much force to splash up onto her sandals. He worked this week to ensure they didn't cross paths. It had been seven days since he'd completely screwed up his life. He only hoped they'd still be able to work together because he didn't know how he'd survive if he lost his best friend, who could chase bad guys on the internet and know exactly what he was thinking.

He heard a car pull up but ignored it. The guys who actually worked the garage could take care of the customer. He loved hanging out here because the garage had always been one of the places he'd felt at home. He'd earned the extra money his family needed by helping his computer teacher in his part-time business which had also introduced him to his teacher's brother who ran a garage. Between the brothers, they'd helped him learn how a man was supposed to act. The work also provided the extra money his mom and his family had needed to survive.

Both the men had sat by his mom at his high school graduation because they'd been just as proud as she was. He hadn't chatted with either of them for a couple of months. He should check in and see if they wanted to come visit the MC. They'd probably welcome a long ride on their bikes.

"Scoop, you have a visitor." Speedy's voice let Scoop know he was probably not going to like the visitor. Speedy had transferred to their Chapter from their Texas Chapter. They'd needed a Road Captain and Speedy had needed to be closer to his aging parents who lived in Wichita. Scoop didn't know him well yet besides that he was a happy guy and enjoyed singing while he worked. War had indicated Bootstrap, the president of the Texas Chapter, had been sad to lose him. He walked through the garage to the reception area, wondering who was looking for him. He stepped in and clocked a woman chatting with Speedy and one of the kids from the high school sitting at the register with a smirk on his face. After the help Scoop had gotten in high school, he'd asked the club to offer spots to teach high school kids about what it takes to be a mechanic. Today was the first week they'd had someone. Scoop walked over to the woman. He figured most men would consider her beautiful, but he didn't notice because even though he'd screwed his life up, his dick still only was interested in Sarah.

"Can I help you?"

She blushed a little but stepped closer. "Umm, well, I was wondering if you'd like to go out sometime. Umm, you can think about it. Here's my number. You can call if you'd like to."

She seemed earnest, but he kept waiting for the punch line. He'd never seen her before in his life, so how'd she know his name and how to find him?

"I'm sorry. Have we met?"

She shook her head. "Not officially, but I saw you last fall at the toy run. When I asked about getting a Property of Scoop keychain, they said they were out, but you were working at the garage if I wanted to see you in person."

"I'm sorry. A Property of Scoop keychain? Where?" He was completely confused, and he had to admit this was one of the weirdest conversations he'd ever had.

"At Regina's Roadside Refuge. I heard they had Property of keychains for the Bluff Creek Brotherhood MC. My friend got a Property of Flick one, but they were out of yours when I went in. So here. Call me if you want to hook up." She held a piece of paper out to him in her hand.

This was surreal, and after he sent her on her way, he was giving his friend Bear a call. When he was upgrading the security system a while back, he'd made it clear that he didn't want anything sold with Property of Scoop on it. He took the paper and watched her walk out to her car, get in, start it up, and leave. As she left the parking lot, Speedy had his phone out and the opening notes to Call Me Maybe came on.

"Turn that off," Scoop growled.

Speedy laughed and started singing the song, dancing around Scoop with the kid joining him. As they sang louder, Baron walked in and started chuckling at them. He loved this song, and they were ruining it for him. It was catchy, and he loved pop, rock from the eighties to early two thousands. He'd never look at this song quite the same again.

Speedy turned the song down a little. "Oh, Scoop, can I wear your property patch? Please?" Speedy's falsetto was impressive, but it didn't make Scoop want to hit him any less.

"Shut up. Baron, did you need something?"

Baron shook his head, walking closer. "Regina saw who was coming to the garage and sent me down here to suggest you close the garage and come to the kitchen for cinnamon rolls. It's looks like I was a little late."

"Yeah, but I sent her on her way. Do you know anything about Property of Scoop keychains?"

Baron laughed, then slapped Scoop on the shoulder. "Regina and Bear have been expanding. You should probably talk with them. You can grab a cinnamon roll while you're there."

Scoop didn't have a good feeling about this, but if Regina was involved, he wouldn't be changing her mind. If she thought it was a good business decision, she'd hold her ground. If nothing else, it had gotten his mind off Sarah and if she'd ever talk to him again. If he wanted to be an adult about it, he'd call and talk with her, but right now, he was choosing to hide out until some of his embarrassment went away.

Now the garage wasn't even a safe place with some jerk at the diner telling women how to find him. If Bear thought him being VP would keep Scoop from kicking him around the ring a little, he was wrong. Cannon had moved up to SAA, and Scoop was happy for his brother. Cannon was tough and had the authoritative attitude to keep everyone in line.

Scoop was happy staying in his little tech world and being the Secretary of the club. The two jobs dovetailed into each other nicely. Scoop was impressed with how Baron and Rascal had been happy to let the younger generation take over. He'd heard all of War's stories while they were working together, but living it was completely different. He wanted his mom and sisters to visit because they'd fall in love with the place. As a traveling nurse, his mom could base herself anywhere, but Baron and Locks' job offer sweetened the deal even more. She and Regina would get along great, and he'd love to have her live close. Both his sisters lived and worked in Dallas. No special reason, but they'd both found jobs there after college. As far as he knew, they didn't have serious guys. They'd made the deal with him that if they got serious, they'd allow him to run their guy's name as an extra layer of security.

And he was back to thinking about Sarah. How was he going to come back from this? Maybe he could take a vacation or hide for the next year so by the time they saw each other, him puking on her shoes wouldn't be so fresh.

He went into the garage bathroom, scrubbing his hands to get the dirt off and splashed his face. Maybe he needed to take his Bronco for a drive. He'd request some time off. He could visit their Texas Chapter and get away from what he'd done. Maybe he'd love it so much that he could stay in Texas long enough that his puking fiasco would be a distant memory.

"Scoop, someone's here to see you!" Speedy yelled through the door. If it was another woman wanting a Property of Scoop keychain, he wasn't sure he could keep his cool.

Drying his hands, he opened the door. Speedy was grinning. "Man, you don't take this one, I'm calling dibs. She's beautiful." He moved his hands, indicating a curvy figure. He didn't know whether he wanted it to be Sarah and face his worst nightmare or someone else. Time to be an adult and face what was waiting for him.

Scoop walked into reception. Sarah was perusing the magazines they had in the area. She was in one of her flowing skirts, a V-neck blouse highlighting her cleavage with her hair down. He glanced at her feet and noticed she had on the sandals she'd worn to the wedding. Either she'd cleaned them or replaced them, but either way, he was fucking embarrassed. Well, looks like it was time to face the music and deal with whatever she was going to tell him. He hoped it wasn't to get the heck out of her life.

"Hey, you asked to see me?" Oh yeah, that was smooth. Could he sound geekier?

"Hey, Rocky Road. I wondered if you and I could talk privately?"

Well, at least she wasn't going to let him down in front of the guys in the garage, and calling him Rocky Road was way better than some name to do with puking.

"Umm, sure. Where would you like?"

"Why don't you come for a drive with me?" Sarah turned and walked out to one of the company SUVs parked by the garage. She cocked an eyebrow, waiting on him. He nodded and slipped off the garage coveralls he'd been wearing, grabbing his wallet and keys from the desk drawer, then followed her out.

"I'm heading out."

He opened the SUV, got in, buckled his seat belt, and took a deep breath. Moment of truth. Sarah's hand reached over, and her fingers rubbed the back of his hand. "Vanilla, relax. Everything's going to be okay."

Sure, she thought it would be okay, but was he going to be okay with what she decided? He took a deep breath, relishing her scent that filled the vehicle. She put it in gear and backed out, turning onto the blacktop.

She flipped the radio on to a country station. She loved her country music. When they were working together, they took turns picking the music. He'd come to appreciate her love of country music, and he hoped she'd come to appreciate the rock and pop music he liked. The silence was killing him.

"I'm sorry I puked on you." Better to get his apology out of the way just in case she never wanted to see him again. She nodded.

"What made you drink that much? I've never seen you drunk before."

How did he answer this without spilling everything? Honestly, at this point, spilling everything seemed the only way to get through all this.

"I used it to get the courage to talk with you about helping me out."

She nodded again and continued driving. Pulling over to the entrance to the dirt track, she put the vehicle in park. She turned toward him. She grinned at him, her lips quirking up at the side.

"Why would you need courage to talk with me? We work together all the time."

He could feel his face getting hot and knew he was blushing. If he ever hated his pale skin and tendency to blush, it was today.

"But I was asking to change that." He waited to see what she'd say. What were her thoughts?

"Well, you're not drunk now so tell me what you want. Spell it out exactly so I know what I'm saying yes or no to."

Oh fuck, she was going to make him ask again. Well, hopefully, if she was making him ask again, she was considering saying yes.

"We have chemistry and we're good friends. I don't want to have my inexperience and virginity hanging over my head. I propose you teach me what I need to know about women."

Sarah's eyes blazed with heat at his words. He might be inexperienced in the act, but he had a lifetime of reading expressions. His eyes trailed down, seeing her pulse pounding in her neck and her nipples harden underneath her blouse. She was interested in what he had to offer. Maybe he hadn't destroyed everything with pukefest.

"So, if we do this, I don't want to be coming to your room at the clubhouse or have you sneaking over to my house. I have two weeks off and I'm going on a road trip. I'm leaving in three days. It would be the perfect way to accomplish your goal without all the brothers getting in our business."

Scoop nodded. He liked her idea because having her alone to himself sounded perfect. They'd be friends with benefits or friends to lovers. But he was going to treat her so good that by the time they returned, she'd want more.

"Okay, when are we leaving so I can request off?"

"Wednesday. I'll send you the itinerary I have so you can add some things you'd like to do." Sarah scooted closer, grasping his T-shirt and pulling him closer. "Let's seal our agreement with a kiss when you're not drunk and you can remember every touch and taste."

The warm touch of her lips against his had his heart pounding. What this woman could do to him with just a kiss. Her lips opened so her tongue swept inside, bringing the taste of a hint of vanilla and coffee. He breathed in her scent, wanting to be closer but not knowing what to do.

Her groan let him know she enjoyed it as much as he did. She pulled back, and he gazed into her eyes, wanting to drown in their depths. Holy hell, if this is what a kiss did to him, what would happen when he finally got inside her?

"I can't wait until we leave. Three days seems like a lifetime."

She turned and grabbed a bag. "If we're going to have me teaching you about women, I think your education wouldn't be complete without a couple romance novels. Read at least one of these before we leave on the trip. I want you to focus specifically on how they treat each other. What makes them think the other person is special and last but certainly not least, how do they talk to each other during sex? I'm clean, but I want us using condoms. You're in charge of getting those. Do you have a preference for what vehicle?"

Wow. He'd known Sarah was organized from when they worked together, but she bullet-pointed the items in a no-nonsense voice that frankly really turned him on.

"I will read these and take care of the condoms. I'd like to take my Bronco if you're okay with that. It's got a hitch just in case I see a vehicle for sale I might want to buy."

She nodded and put the vehicle back in gear. "Sounds good. My sisters know what is going on because I needed their opinions, but they won't be sharing with anyone. Not even their husbands."

"I'll request vacation, but no one needs to know our plans. Do you want me to pick you up, or should we have a meeting place?"

"Let me think about that. I wouldn't put it past Locks to try to make Jesse put a tracker on my vehicle."

She pulled up in front of the garage and turned toward him. "I'll do this, Rocky Road, as long as it doesn't change our friendship. You're one of the few people who don't irritate me when we're working together. I'm not losing that."

He nodded. He'd never do anything to hurt her, but what if they could be so much more than friends? "Promise."

He closed his door and watched her back out. He needed to get to reading, but he hid a smile. She'd never been in his room, so she didn't know how much of a bibliophile he was. Growing up, his mom, his sisters and he went to the library weekly to stock up. Sometimes, he'd run out of books before it was time to go back, so he'd read a couple of his mom's favorites. One had such an impact; he'd had the quote inked on his skin. He couldn't wait to see Sarah's face when she saw it and wondered if she'd recognize it. Maybe her taste in romance novels would give him insight into how to win her heart. What exactly spoke to his woman because he wanted her for more than just sex, though he was anticipating getting her naked. Two weeks to savor the woman he couldn't get off his mind in every way possible. He was a fast learner and had no doubt Sarah would be an excellent teacher. After he had her sated and happy, he'd work on convincing her she was the woman of his dreams, and they could have it all.

Chapter Four

War was back from his honeymoon and had scheduled a council meeting since Scoop was getting ready to leave for two weeks. War had explained to him that Bluff Creek called it council because Regina put her foot down about calling it church. Since she volunteered at the church, she said it was confusing. Baron would do anything for Regina, so they called it council. Scoop dropped his phone in the basket at the entrance to the meeting room and found his seat at the table.

He felt a little bad about leaving for two weeks, but he wasn't giving up this chance with Sarah. Flick sat down beside him and immediately opened up a breakfast burrito from the diner. The smell wafted over and had Scoop's stomach growling.

Flick took a bite, then grabbed two boxes and pushed them toward the middle of the table, flipping the lids open. The wonderful smell was stronger. Scoop reached in and grabbed one for himself before they were gone.

"So now we're having snacks at council?" War grunted while reaching his hand toward the box.

"Thought you'd be in a better mood after your honeymoon. Pres, you don't have to eat one if you don't agree with me bringing them to share."

Scoop had to listen closely since Flick was speaking around a huge bite of burrito he was chewing.

"Smartass. I'm in a fantastic mood, not that it's any of you assholes' business."

"I think if you're going to be grumpy, I'm going to tell Phoebe on you. I know you're not on the monthly plan," Baron retorted.

"What monthly plan?"

"Well, thanks to the Franks sisters, Phoebe, Grant and David have come up with a monthly fee you can pay to the swear jar."

War shook his head. "I don't know whether to be impressed or worried what they'll come up with next."

"My granddaughter will rule the world, and I'm going to help her do it." Rascal's grin was the widest Scoop had ever seen.

"Our granddaughter," Locks grunted.

"Whatever, our granddaughter. You're a little cranky in your old age."

"Quit calling me old. I'm well-seasoned."

Scoop laughed along with the other guys. Although Locks and Rascal sniping at each other was funny, he knew War had things to accomplish.

"Let's see if we can get the agenda done and then you all can continue your whining."

Scoop wasn't the only one hiding his smile at their glares.

"Okay, Scoop will be out of pocket for a couple of weeks. Our Texas Chapter has offered to take care of any tech or hacking needs, but let's try to keep it to a minimum. Maybe for once, we could have a qui…"

"Shut up!" Baron yelled. "Don't you dare jinx us."

"Yeah, I don't need that type of crap right now," Cannon muttered.

War held his hands out. "Okay, calm your tits."

"I don't fucking have tits," Cannon growled.

"Well, technically, you have nipples on your chest but that's not where the phrase came from," Flick mentioned around another mouthful of food.

"As interesting as this conversation is, let's get back to the matter at hand. How's the diner doing?"

Bear pulled out a spreadsheet and slid his reading glasses on. "We've maintained steady traffic and haven't seen a dip in sales. We've added a couple of new promotional items and maybe that's helping."

Scoop had a bone to pick with Bear. He was guessing one of the items was the freaking Property of Scoop keychains.

"Yeah, did we ever agree to allow our road names on merchandise?" Scoop questioned, glaring at the grin spreading across the man who used to be the grumpy SAA.

"Yes, we did. When you all approved me ordering whatever merchandise I wanted to for the diner. If you have a problem, I could use a workout. Want to meet me in the ring at my wife's gym?"

Scoop hadn't been in the ring in a long time and Bear actively worked out at the gym. Besides, he didn't want to hurt anything he'd need when he and Sarah left on their trip.

"I don't think we need to meet in the ring because I disagree with someone giving out the information about where I was working. Then I had to deal with one of your customers coming to the garage to give me her number."

Scoop knew he'd let his anger show, but telling someone his whereabouts wasn't only not cool but also not safe for them. If Bear didn't understand the gravity of that, then they were going to have problems.

"Woah. Say what?"

"A female customer stopped by the garage to give me her number. Someone at Regina's Roadside Refuge had told her how to find me."

Bear scribbled a note on his paper. "I'm so sorry, Scoop. We hired a couple of high school seniors to work in the gift shop part of the diner in the evenings. I guess I didn't even think not telling customers how to find one of the brothers needed to be part of their orientation, but I'll take care of it as soon as our meeting is over."

"Thanks, Bear."

Scoop listened to the rest of the meeting, not contributing much. His mind was already on his trip with Sarah. Sure, he couldn't wait for her to teach him about sex, but it was so much more than that.

He wanted to spend the time with her, getting to know her hopes and dreams. Did she want kids? As nurturing as she was, he couldn't imagine her without a couple of kids. It was too soon for him to imagine they were his, but man, he wanted them to be. Maybe they'd go on the trip, and he'd find out she wasn't like he thought, but he doubted it.

Working with her since he'd come to the MC had given him a pretty good idea of her personality. What he'd experienced had him wanting more.

"Okay, one thing I need you all to consider is we're stretched pretty thin. We need a couple new prospects. Roam, Bear, and I have a couple of friends from the military dropping by while Scoop's out of pocket. I think they'd be a good fit. I'll have Scoop check them out before he leaves, but if you're in town next week, I want your take on them. Now, get out of here. I'm meeting Remington for lunch."

Flick laughed along with a couple of other brothers. "Is that what we're calling it? Lunch at 10:45 a.m.?"

Scoop had to admit he'd thought the same thing, but War was in a fantastic mood and there was no way Scoop was ticking him off today. Flick was either feeling brave or stupid.

"Yes, if you have to know. With all the freakin' animals around here, Remi thinks she'd like something. We're driving to Dodge City because Whiskey says he has a friend who rescues animals."

"Oh man, I hope she falls in love with this itty bitty frou frou dog that becomes your best friend, War."

Scoop didn't know why his brothers were antagonizing War, but he just wanted to get out of there before Cannon or Flick screwed up the day.

"Cannon, when you finally find someone who makes every day better, you'll understand that I would do just about anything to make her smile. Now, get out of here. We're done."

Scoop grabbed his phone as he slipped out the door. He had some packing and planning to do.

Chapter Five

S arah had arranged to have them meet in Wichita. Jesse had to pick up an SUV, and Sarah had offered to drop her off at the start of her trip. What Sarah thought Locks didn't know was that Jesse was picking up the SUV, then following Sarah to one of the security company's safe houses not in use. Sarah's SUV would stay in the garage, and Jesse would deliver Sarah to Scoop.

They were meeting in a gas station parking lot because Sarah said she'd wanted to get a couple snacks before they left. He'd looked at her itinerary and only had a couple places to add. Besides shopping for the Fiestaware she was interested in and checking out some other places of interest, he wanted them to experience dates.

He'd found a place to go dancing, and when he knew for sure where they were staying on some of the overnights, he'd add some other activities. Sarah's sisters had been texting non-stop. He looked at his phone when it pinged again.

Remington: We're trusting you with her. Don't screw it up.

Winchester: She's really looking forward to going away. She thinks we don't know about the book signing, but I'm snoopy. It's a huge deal she's letting you go with her. MAKE IT SPECIAL.

Beth: She's going to a book signing and teaching nerdy boy about sex. How is that fair?

His face heated knowing all the sisters knew how inexperienced he was. If only his face didn't show every embarrassing thing he felt. Besides being good at tech, he'd liked not having to deal with embarrassing situations when he was a beat cop. He'd been so glad when he'd gotten assigned to the security and technical division after he completed his rookie assignment.

Scoop: You guys remember I'm in this group text, right?

Beth: Yeah, but if you can't take a little ribbing about sex, then you have no business dating our sister.

Remington: Even though I'm the oldest, Sarah shouldered a lot, especially with Dad, when Mom died. She deserves a break. Also, besides collecting Fiestaware, she collects magnets for her fridge. You're welcome.

Scoop: Gotta go. She's coming to the car.

Remington: Good luck. Code Janice.

Winchester: You got this. Code Janice.

Beth: Have fun. Code Janice.

Scoop hopped out to help Sarah with her bags. She had a cooler, which he added to the back seat near the one he'd brought, a bag, a backpack, and her computer case. She was scrumptious today. She had on a body-hugging T-shirt which cupped her breasts and was tucked into a well-washed pair of jeans which were white in places from so many washings. Cute tennis shoes rounded out her outfit. Her hair was down around her shoulders, with the blonde strands blowing in the light breeze. She placed her sweatshirt along with a baseball cap with the bail bonds logo on it between them on the seat. He'd heard her lamenting one time to her sisters how it wasn't fair she had their mom's figure. She was shorter than Winchester and Remington, who were lean and muscled whereas, at five foot five, Sarah was perfect as far as he was concerned. Rounded, lush, and womanly. She settled in, her fresh and light scent he adored surrounding him, and opened the bag in her hand.

"Sucker?" Sarah held out a bag of Tootsie pops. Sarah had the habit of chewing on pencils or pens. When she'd visited the dentist last time, she had been told to stop. He'd only known about it because she'd been fuming over it when they were working on a project. Beth had decided to help her by buying her a huge bag of Tootsie Roll Pops. Seriously. He was going to have to watch her suck on lollipops for the whole trip. He hadn't even considered this. When they were searching for information the last time after she'd quit chewing the pens, she'd had a sucker in her mouth. The bulge of the lollipop in her cheek made him think of other things making her cheek bulge out a little. Most of the time, she was in her computer cave at the bail bonds building and he was in his at the MC clubhouse. Listening to her suck on them was bad enough, but watching her do it was excruciating. She unwrapped a grape one, licked across it, and then had it in her mouth while she was waiting. Her tongue moved it to the side and her mouth moved while she tasted it. She pulled it out a little, ran her tongue around it again, then sucked it inside her mouth. Did she have no idea what it did to him or any man watching her tongue the sucker?

"Scoop, I'm not holding the bag forever."

"Umm, I'm okay. Maybe later." Yeah, maybe after he could get his dick to quit pressing against his zipper. He fought himself. He wanted to adjust and get a little relief against his dick, but Sarah's big blue eyes were watching him. Focus on the road trip now. Taste every inch of her later including her mouth. She probably tasted like the grape sucker she had in her mouth. Obviously, since he'd made it to thirty-five years, a person couldn't expire from sexual frustration, but this trip might change that. He'd never been hard freaking twenty-four-seven.

"So, straight up 135?" He put on his blinker and pulled out onto the road. Concentrate on driving and the feel of the steering wheel in his hands. Ignore the sweet scent of grape drifting over toward him. Fuckety-fuck-fuck. He didn't want to wreck because he wasn't paying attention, but it was impossible to not imagine her lips wrapped around his dick instead of the sucker. He'd never had a blow job, but the book Sarah had him read had described it. Oh, had described it. He'd had to rub one out after reading it because there was no way he could have fallen asleep.

"Yep. We're heading up to Lindsborg to see their Main Street. It's a Swedish community and they have crafts and food items that are Swedish themed. I've always wanted a Dala horse. Then I want to see Coronado Heights. Next on to the motorcycle museum in Marquette and then back on the highway to Oklahoma unless you wanted to stop somewhere else."

"All right. Let's get this trip started." Maybe he'd survive this, but it was going to be painful. If he could keep his emotions in check when he hated his police chief, then surely, he could hide his need from Sarah for a couple of hours in the car.

Sarah fiddled with her phone and his radio. He'd installed Bluetooth so he could choose what he listened to. The strains of "Walking in Memphis" came through the speakers.

"Good choice."

Sarah grinned, "Glad you like it. You know country is my jam."

"And I'm rock, pop from about anytime, and ABBA because my mom's a huge ABBA fan so we can share the music. How's that sound?"

Sarah bopped in her seat to the music, humming along and singing every once in a while. He kept his eyes on the road when all he wanted to do was watch her. This trip would either be the best thing he'd ever experienced or break his heart into little pieces if she didn't feel the same about him. He tapped his fingers along the steering wheel.

He had the cruise control on, but he couldn't keep still. So much was riding on this trip. Sure, he'd said it was about teaching him about sex, and it was, but he wanted more from her.

Sarah's hand slid over onto his thigh and patted it. "Scoop, I can tell you're freaking out. How about we pretend to be new boyfriend and girlfriend? I have a list of things you'll be learning, but if it makes it easier, pretend each thing we do is a separate date."

He glanced over at her gorgeous eyes, reassuring him everything would be okay. He nodded because he wasn't sure he could form the words. His face heated. Just once, could he not fucking blush?

THEY'D GONE AND VISITED so many shops on Main Street in Lindsborg. He'd loved them, but he loved watching

Sarah's face light up with each new thing they found more. He'd bought a T-shirt from the same shop Sarah bought a Dala horse with *Welcome* on it. She'd talked about the origin of them and that they were horses because horses were such a valued item. It was a cute red-orange color. He would have bought one for his mom if she had a home, but he didn't see any way it would hang on her RV.

Now he and Sarah were heading to Coronado Heights. He was interested to see what it was. He passed the old cemetery with big signs stating it wasn't the entrance to Coronado Heights. He made the turn and his Bronco bumped along the road. The twists and turns were tight because they were climbing three hundred feet within a small space. He hoped no one was coming down because the road was tight and there wasn't room for a car to pass.

"This is a little steep, but it's interesting how it's in the middle of the prairie. Do you know its history?" Sarah leaned forward as if it would help her see around the curve they were driving.

"I hoped my tour guide would tell me."

Sarah giggled. "I've got you covered, Rocky Road. So it's believed near here is where Francisco Vasquez de Coronado gave up his search for the seven cities of gold and turned to return to Mexico. In 1915, a professor at Bethany College found a piece of woven metal thought to be Spanish chain mail at the Sharps Creek site. There was a Native American village excavation site a few miles southwest of the hill. In 1936, a WPA project built the stone castle to commemorate the site."

"WPA was the works project to build infrastructure and get us out of the Great Depression, wasn't it?"

"Yes, Hoover Dam was one of the projects, too."

Scoop rounded the last turn and saw the area. Stone picnic tables and large stone fireplaces dotted the hill.

"Okay if I park here?" He motioned to beside the stone castle. Sarah nodded with a huge smile on her face. He parked and grabbed his jacket. "Lead the way."

Sarah was out of the Bronco and waiting for him to come around the front. "Oh, look at the path. Did they put picnic areas built into the side of the hill?"

Scoop motioned toward them. "Let's go see." He kept close by to see if Sarah wanted help. The path was rocky. Even the parking areas were just dirt and gravel. He glanced around. If he had to guess, he'd estimate the whole plateau was about the size of one football field. Yucca plants and some grasses native to Kansas were about three feet high in areas. He followed her to the edge of the hill. "Oh, wow."

Small picnic areas were built into the side of the hill. The path toward them was mostly covered. He'd do whatever Sarah wanted, but he wondered how many snakes were hiding in those areas. Kansas had plenty of snakes that were harmless, but there were some he didn't want to run into.

"Do you want to walk down there or stay up here?"

"I'm good with up here." She tightened her jacket around her as they walked toward the other picnic area. She shivered. He slid his arm around her because she said to act as if this was a date. He figured it was okay because he couldn't imagine allowing a date to shiver without trying to fix it. She snuggled under his arm.

"It's amazing to me that it was calm walking down the streets, but up here, it's colder and so much windier."

Scoop relished the feel of her in his arms and enjoyed the moment. He was thankful for the wind since it got Sarah in his arms. He could see for miles. A stream ran beside the hill. The landscape was dotted with farms, and a dirt road bisected the area, heading to what he thought was south.

"Yeah, if you were picnicking up here, you'd need to weigh down your plates. Should we check out the castle?"

Sarah nodded. He kept his arm around her as they walked toward the castle. It looked about twenty feet high and was made from large red and brown stones. They entered the main area. Scoop looked around at the cement floors and rock tables. Part of the floor looked newer so at some point it must have been re-done. The table legs were made of the same stones and mortar as the outside of the castle. The tops of the tables and benches were cement. A couple of walls had graffiti someone had painted. A stone fireplace had branches and burned logs. He wondered if kids from the town came out here and partied.

"Oh, look! Let's check out the stairs." He followed behind Sarah, enjoying the view of her butt in the jeans. She glanced back and caught him looking. He could feel the heat in his face as he blushed. Why couldn't he be like the brothers in the MC, who even if they got embarrassed, didn't have their faces showing everything?

She patted his arm as they paused on the roof of the structure. "You don't need to be embarrassed about checking out my ass, Vanilla. I'm glad you like mine. It makes me feel sexy, and I certainly enjoy looking at yours."

He gazed at her smirk as the wind blew her hair across her lush lips. He tucked the strands behind her ear and was heartily glad she'd given the go ahead to act like they were dating. "Does it make you feel even sexier knowing everything you do turns me on?" He wanted to slide his hand around her neck and tug her toward him. She must have read his mind because she leaned down and claimed his lips. It was just as perfect as the first time, but this time, he let himself enjoy the way she made him feel. Sarah stepped closer until she was flush against him. Her breasts pressed against him. Yep, it was official. He was going to spend the whole trip hard because everything she did had him ready to blast off. He wasn't sure when she planned for them to finally have sex, but he didn't think getting to be inside her would help with his hard-on long term. Once he'd experienced her pussy clamping around him, he'd just want more. At least that's what all the books he read said, and he could believe it. One taste, one touch, would never be enough with Sarah.

Voices from downstairs had them pulling apart. He didn't want to scar some family who'd come to visit the castle. His hand reached for Sarah's, intertwining their fingers.

"On to Marquette?"

"Yep, we've got a schedule to keep."

He followed her down the stairs and back to his Bronco. He'd been apprehensive about the trip, but now, he was wondering if two weeks was enough time to spend with her. He'd just have to use the time to convince her that she couldn't live without him.

Chapter Six

Sarah squirmed in the seat, shifting to alleviate her nervousness. She'd had a perfect day with Scoop. He was attentive and funny, and they could talk about anything. Their topics had ranged from movies to books they liked and then on to new computer items they had on their wish lists.

They'd even started singing along with the radio which she loved to do. Scoop had an amazing voice which did things to her she wasn't quite ready for on the trip. His voice was deep when he talked, but when he sang, it sent shivers down her spine. Trying to keep him from noticing had been a trial.

Their first overnight stop was at a casino in Tonkawa. When she'd been planning the trip, she'd worried how long they'd spend at the museum and the attractions. She hadn't wanted to drive four or five hours after they left Wichita, so she'd chosen the casino. Plus, one of the MC members enjoyed gambling and had a free night coupon flyer that Scoop had grabbed before being seen.

The closer they drove to the casino, the more nervous she became. Her stomach was churning. She'd imagined having Scoop in bed so many times. He starred in her dreams and in her imagination for months before he'd asked for her help. Whenever she pulled her trusty battery-operated boyfriend out, Scoop had been who she pictured.

What if they didn't have the chemistry she imagined? Their kiss had swamped her senses, but what if when they finally had each other, it fell flat? Plus, the added weight of teaching him. When she and her sisters were discussing it, the idea seemed sexy. Now, she was flat out worried and heading into downright petrified of changing their relationship.

She chatted with Scoop usually daily, and the last week when he was avoiding her was horrible. What if, after they had their time together, not only did they not become more, but he dropped her as a friend completely? Scoop's voice drew her out of her thoughts.

"You know we don't have to do anything tonight besides sleep beside each other. I reserved a king bed, and we don't even have to touch if you're not ready. I'm enjoying spending time with you on the trip. When it happens, it happens. No pressure."

She turned to see Scoop's face lit by the dashboard lights. Once they'd crossed the Kansas/Oklahoma border, the lights were few and far between.

"How'd you know I was nervous?"

He grinned, glancing toward her, then back to the road. "You twirl your hair when you're thinking or nervous. If your hair's up in a bun, you twirl your pencil. When you're deeply thinking, you chew on something or suck on your lollipops."

Seemed he knew her pretty well. She had a list, but now, the list was seeming so cold and calculating. She was so confused, and it wasn't like her. She was a planner. It's one of the reasons she was so good at her job. She planned for all eventualities, but she was in unknown territory. Her previous times having sex were with people she'd dated for a while. Her last one was the engineer and honestly, he couldn't find a clit if it had a huge arrow pointing toward it. He'd been a tweak to her nipple, slide his finger down to see if she was wet, which hello, didn't happen after the first time and then slam, bam, not even a thank you ma'am.

The first time she'd thought it might be a fluke how fast he'd been, and she'd been wet because he'd been kissing her and fondling her through her clothes. Her expectations had been raised and then, poof, he was one and done. She'd decided to give him another chance because she did like him, and he was a nice guy. After the second time, she'd realized not only couldn't he find her clit, but he also didn't care to. He'd yelled when she'd broken up with him, saying how she couldn't find anyone better. Hello, her b.o.b. was better because he didn't disappoint before the big finish.

Which is why she was nervous to teach Scoop. She'd had sex with three men and only one of them had made it worth her while. How was she going to teach him if she wasn't sure what she liked? But she had promised, and she didn't go back on her word.

"Let me go grab our key, and then I'll be back."

She watched Scoop walk into the office, then pulled out her list. She'd listed the erogenous zones, and she considered them way more than the seven the Friends episode had talked about. First on the list is teaching him about one through six.

She'd wait until they'd showered tonight, then they'd experience the zones, and they'd both also experience not completing. One of the things she'd realized is Scoop had missed out on all those things most high school kids experienced.

He hadn't made out in a car, touching over clothes only to stop before the finish. It wasn't just the actual act of sex and a blow job he'd missed out on. She had two weeks to give him all the experiences he'd missed and teach him to rival even the best book boyfriend she'd read about. She'd follow her plan and make this perfect for him.

SHE'D SHOWERED FIRST, and Scoop was in there now. He'd gazed at her before he went in and reiterated he'd follow her lead.

She wondered if he'd be irritated that they weren't just holding each other, they were going to do a little touching and be very sexually frustrated if it went the way she envisioned. She was under the covers, wearing her cotton pajamas. The long pants had computer code on them. She'd matched it with a cotton turquoise tank top.

She had her readers on and had her e-reader open, but she wasn't reading. The book was great, but she couldn't concentrate imagining Scoop under the water. She hadn't ever seen him with his shirt off. She was curious if he was covered in tattoos or had virgin skin. She assumed he had the Bluff Creek MC logo because most of the guys did, but it wasn't a requirement.

The door opened, and she'd swear her heart stopped. Holy Hotness! Scoop was running a towel over his hair to dry it. Gray pajama pants hung low on his hips. His chest was defined and had a thin arrow of hair which trailed down to his waistband where he had the v she'd only read about. She ached to trace her tongue along there, but nope, not tonight. Licking that wasn't on her menu of experiences yet. Later, definitely later.

A tattoo she couldn't read the words to was directly under his right pec. She swallowed. Her belly tightened. Everything about him turned her on. Right now, she didn't care that she was six years older. Something about Scoop called to her. When they were together, she felt complete.

"What's your tattoo say?"

He grinned and walked closer. He'd missed a couple drops of water on his chest. If they were farther along, she'd totally lick those drops of water off, but for now, patience was needed.

"It's from one of my mom's favorite books by Julie Garwood. I got it before I joined the police academy because it reminds me one person can make a difference."

Sarah slid her finger toward it, then gazed at him for permission. He grasped her hand and placed her finger at the first word. *One whisper, added to a thousand others, becomes a roar of discontent.*

"What book?" She asked as her finger traced each word.

"The Secret. It's one of her historical romances. I read them all because I'd run out of books before we'd go back to the library. I always like the battles in the books."

"I love the quote. It shows we can make a difference."

He nodded and turned off the lights. Pulling the covers back, he crawled into bed and scooted close to her. She laid her e-reader and glasses on the nightstand. He situated himself on his pillow and held his arm out, inviting her to lay on his shoulder.

She shook her head and flicked the light back on. "So, tonight's lesson is on erogenous zones. I know you thought we weren't doing anything, but I didn't want you too nervous."

His cheeks flushed, and his breathing sped up. She smiled. Oh yes, Scoop was on board with it.

"Okay, what's first?" he croaked. She hid her smile because she didn't want him to misconstrue how cute she thought he was.

"So many times, people forget there are multiple places that turn us on. There are so many nerve endings. We're starting with six of my favorite and they are all neck and above."

Scoop sat up and leaned back against the headboard. "What's first?"

"So, I'm going to illustrate the zones, then you get to try them out on me."

She slid closer, raising her finger to his cheek and running it over his lips. "So many people think the lips are the only place, but there are so many more places."

Her hand slid around his neck, tracing along the back of his neck while she leaned close to his ear, then nibbled on his earlobe.

HOLY FUCK! HOW WAS he supposed to learn from Sarah when he could barely concentrate? Her lips had nibbled along his ear, then her warm breath had followed. The shivers going down his spine had him wondering if he'd survive this trip, but if not, what a way to go. He wouldn't have thought his eyebrows or eyelids were things that would turn him on, but her lips and fingers whispering across them had him fighting not to come.

She hadn't even touched his dick. Hell, she hadn't touched anything below his neck. Her lips ghosting up the side of his neck had him fighting not to touch her, but she instructed him no touches until it was his turn.

If he didn't concentrate on something else, the sensations would overwhelm him.

"Stop," he groaned.

"Why?" she whispered against his ear, licking the shell.

"Because I'm so hard I could pound nails, and I'm so ready to blow."

She leaned back with the biggest grin on her face. She was enjoying how hot she made him, and he wanted to return the favor.

"Well, how about you practice what you've learned, if it will help you cool down, but remember, nobody comes tonight."

He nodded his head, knowing this wouldn't be the first time with Sarah he'd end the night sexually frustrated, but it would be worth it to have the opportunity to touch and taste her skin even if it was only her neck and above.

She leaned back against the headboard as he had, and he scooted closer. He started to place his hand on her shoulder, then realized that was one of the off-limits places. Instead, he lifted her hair, sliding his finger lightly along her neck like she'd done to him. He leaned closer, trying to mimic how lightly she'd nibbled his ear. He focused on her reactions because if he didn't, he'd be swept away by how it felt touching and tasting her skin. She shivered when his breath ghosted close to her ear and his tongue tasted her earlobe.

Her hands started to move toward his chest, but she stopped herself. He grinned, knowing what he was doing was turning her on. He ghosted his lips across her cheeks, caressing her eyebrows and placing a kiss against her closed eyelids. She shivered and groaned.

How had he not known how thrilling it was watching a woman he wanted give herself over to the pleasure? Maybe because no one had ever fascinated him like Sarah.

The first time he'd noticed her was when she'd questioned his name and started calling him ice cream flavors. Even though the attention had embarrassed him, she'd mesmerized him. When he'd realized she was their tech person, she'd enticed him even more.

He slid his lips along her jaw while trailing his fingers along her neck, drawing patterns. Her lips slid open, and he grinned against her skin.

Each touch and taste had him wanting more, but the parameters she'd placed actually helped. He could savor how soft her skin was and the faint hint of vanilla that tempted him to lean closer.

He slid his hand up, clasping her face and then tasted her lips. Following the example she'd set, he slid his tongue lightly against her open mouth, tracing her lips, and then he dove in. Her tongue stroking and tangling against his had him grasping the hair along her nape, turning her head for a better angle.

He focused on the faint taste of the cherry sucker she'd had earlier to keep from focusing on his dick, his hard-as-nails, ready to explode in his pajama pants dick. He pulled away to nibble on her ear and to breathe deeper. Kissing Sarah took his breath away and had him thinking of more than just kissing and caressing tonight.

Sarah's hand sliding up to his face and her finger sliding up to his lips had him stopping to look at her.

"You feel incredible and are a fast learner. We need to stop, or I'll throw my plan out the window."

He chuckled, cocking his eyebrow. At this point, he'd be fine with throwing the plan out the window and tasting the creamy skin of her breasts which were close to spilling out of her tank top.

"Nope, you're sexy as all get out, Scoop, but I, I mean, *we* have a plan. Now, lie down and let me snuggle against your shoulder tonight because that's what boyfriends and girlfriends do, right?"

Scoop slid down in the bed, holding his arm out for Sarah to snuggle against his shoulder. She scooted closer and snuggled against him. He flicked off the light. Maybe sharing about his family with Sarah would help him calm down. He wanted a hope of sleeping tonight.

"I've met your sisters. Have I told you about mine?"

"No," she whispered. Having Sarah's warm breath waft across his chest and her arm laid over him was a glimpse of what they could have.

"So, I was ten when they were born. Dad left a week after Mom had them."

Sarah jerked her head up off his chest. "What?"

Scoop loved she was outraged for him, but it had been a long time ago. He slid his hand into her hair, settling her back against his shoulder.

"Yeah, he was an ass. He wanted more boys and decided he didn't want to be a dad after they were born. Not that he was that great before. He wanted to show people he was a good dad in public, but in private, I was a nuisance. He just packed up and left. Mom had been going to school to become a nurse and suddenly money was tight. It's how I got into computers and cars. One of my teachers and his brother taught me. I also babysat when I could so Mom could continue attending classes. Tasha and Rose are twenty-five now. Rose is a police officer in Texas and Tasha is a nurse in the same city. I'll probably call them on our trip. I usually check in every one to two weeks. It was before the wedding the last time I talked to them. Rose's name fits her perfectly. She's this gorgeous, strong woman, but man, you have to get past the thorns to be gifted with the amazing woman underneath. She's had a little trouble at work because she can outshoot most of the older officers."

Sarah giggled, "Umm, yeah, I can understand that."

"I bet you can. So many of the guys underestimate you and your sisters, then bam, you all kick their ass."

"What about Tasha? Is that short for anything?"

"Natasha, but she prefers Tasha, plus Rose couldn't say Natasha when they were little. Like I said, she's a nurse. She likes the excitement of the different cases in the ER. She tried labor and delivery, but she said she couldn't handle when the babies didn't make it."

"That would be hard."

Scoop breathed deep, enjoying Sarah in his arms. She was the whole package, and he wasn't sure how he'd give her up when the trip was over.

Chapter Seven

S coop followed the directions on the signs at the Drive-In Theater. He'd never been to a drive-in and thought it sounded fun, but Sarah already had it on her list of 'experiences' for him. If they were in public, he was guessing this would be another time where he ended the evening frustrated. When he'd brought it up this morning about having a hard time going to sleep last night, she'd giggled, freaking giggled at him. Then she'd grasped his hard cock through his pajamas and said he'd missed all this in high school, and if he got to come, then he'd miss out on some of the frustration of high school.

Sarah was taking this teaching him seriously. When he'd asked her, he'd envisioned her directing him to what she liked with lots and lots of sex together. This trip was nothing like he imagined, but he was having the best time of his life.

He'd finally touched base with Tasha and Rose this morning while Sarah was in the shower. He needed something to keep his mind off the water sliding all over her naked body he hadn't seen but had no problem imagining. Rose had told him she was handling the issues at her work and denied she needed his help. Tasha had said she loved him and would call him some other time. She was coming off twenty-four hours at the hospital and needed sleep.

He'd texted his mom to see if she'd had time to review what the MC had sent. She said she was on a shift and couldn't talk. She'd been in contact with Baron and Regina and said she was considering it if he really wouldn't mind his mother that close.

Wouldn't mind? He'd love to have his mother that close. Now, if he could convince Rose and Tasha to move closer, life would be almost perfect.

"Oh, how about right here, Scoop? I don't want too far to walk to the bathroom during the movies."

Scoop gave Sarah all his attention and pulled into the space. She'd already indicated they were to face the screen which seemed kind of strange. He'd researched online and a lot of people parked backwards and sat in the back of their trucks with blow-up mattresses or lawn chairs. He'd go along with whatever Sarah said. She hadn't let him down so far.

"Okay, I did a mix of what my mom used to do and of what I wanted. We have bottles of the drinks we both like because although I love fountain drinks, the price is ridiculous. I've got Tootsie Pops for me and beef jerky for you. Let's go grab some popcorn and anything else you see. We've got a little bit before the show starts."

He got out and walked around the truck to open Sarah's door. If they were playing boyfriend and girlfriend, he'd told her to wait in the truck until he opened her door. Her smile lit something inside him.

He opened her door, holding his hand out to help her. Her warm palm placed in his had him wanting to pull her closer for a kiss. Fuck it! Maybe it wasn't in the plans, but her lips glistened with the vanilla-flavored gloss she preferred. He stepped closer, leaned down and brushed his lips against hers.

Nothing too deep to scar any families waiting for the movie, even though he considered it a little racy for little kids. Her lips clung to his as he pulled away. He wasn't sure how one person could make him happy by just being with him.

"Lead the way to the snacks."

His mom had taught him how to treat a woman, but having her go in front of him was a little self-serving. Her rounded ass cupped by her jeans was one of his favorite features of hers. He couldn't wait until he could finally see it without any clothes obstructing his view. He clicked the remote to lock his Bronco and followed his pseudo-girlfriend.

SARAH SIPPED HER WATER and waited for the next movie to start. It was a double feature and a good number of cars had left as the first movie ended.

"You said you all used to come to the movies together?"

Scoop's words pulled her out of thinking about what was next.

"Yes, at times the grief from losing her feels like it was yesterday, but the ten-year anniversary is coming up. We wouldn't have survived the first few years without the MC."

Scoop's hand reached over and clasped hers. "Sorry, I didn't mean to make you sad."

Sarah shook her head. "You didn't... that much. It's not as raw as it was originally, but big milestones bring it front and center again. Remi getting married. Winnie becoming a mom."

"I'm sorry you all won't have her at all the special occasions."

Scoop's kind words brought home how much her mom would have loved him.

"She loved that we were part of the business, but she always reminded us to also find our one. She said despite the fact that she loved her job, her life was complete when she had us, even though she lamented many times she wouldn't have minded a boy."

"A boy?"

Sarah smiled at the memory. "When Remi started dating and came home upset after a date, Mom said she wished she would have had one boy first to be the protective older brother. Mom never knew that Dad called Roam to go kick the boy's ass."

"Roam but not War?"

"Oh no, War had already been an ass. Roam was always a friend to Remi."

"Do you think your dad will be single the rest of his life?"

"I hope not. Remi and I pulled him aside about a year ago and made sure he knew we'd be on board with him dating. Beth had told us she thought she spotted him out with a woman when she was in Dodge City. We didn't want him to have to hide it. He told us no one would ever be Mom. Remi tried to explain we understood no one would be Mom, but Mom wouldn't want him alone forever either. He just walked out of the room and didn't talk to us for a week."

"That has to be hard because we want our family to be happy."

Sarah nodded. So far, they'd watched the movie, but she had other plans for the next feature. Time to get them back on track. She was introducing Scoop to heavy petting on top of their clothes and maybe a little grinding. She'd play it out and see. She placed her water in the holder and scooted a little closer.

Scoop turned toward her, his eyes dipping down to her cleavage, highlighted by her V-neck. She slid her fingers up his arm to his shoulders.

Leaning close to him, she breathed in his scent, woodsy with the smell of leather, one of her favorite scents.

"Tonight, we're going to experience zones seven through eleven, but we can't slide fingers or mouths under any clothes."

Scoop slid his arm along the back of the bench seat. "What are zones seven through eleven?"

His breathing picked up a little. She hoped his breathing would speed up even more. She glided her fingers across his chest toward his collarbone. "Seven is the collarbone."

Her fingers slid over his shoulder, then down his arm. "This is the only one that can touch skin. Eight is the underside of the arm."

She trailed her fingers around his wrist, then softly drew circles and swirls up the underside of his arm. Scoop shivered as her finger slid across his bicep. His eyes blazed with heat, and they hadn't really started yet.

She scooted until their hips were touching. "Nine and ten are the breasts and nipples."

Her fingers accompanied her words as she slid both hands across his pecs and then scratched her fingernails on the outside of the shirt over his nipples. Scoop's nostrils flared and his mouth opened a little.

"Can only my fingers touch your breasts and nipples, or can my mouth?"

Sarah tilted her head and considered his request. "You can use your mouth, but if the skin isn't already uncovered, then you have to touch only through clothing."

Scoop nodded and turned more fully toward her. His fingers followed the path hers had along her collarbone, then on the outside of her arm. When his fingers went around her wrist and started up the underside of her arm, she wondered how the hell she was going to handle this. Scoop's touch had all thoughts of teaching him leaving her head.

She shivered as her nipples hardened when his fingers grazed the underside of her elbow, then up her arm.

Scoop paused, looking at her, then at the steering wheel. "I want to be closer, but I'm not sure how." His face flushed.

"Let's slide the bench seat back, then I'll show you."

He quickly slid the lever, moving the seat back. She motioned him to scoot into the middle of the bench. When he was there, she slid one thigh over his, then settled her ass on his thighs. She didn't have her core over his cock because she wanted to see what Scoop would do.

He swallowed, then brought his hand up to cup her breast through her bra and shirt. He lifted one and squeezed lightly, causing everything inside her to heat up.

Chapter Eight

Scoop worked to not lose it all at the feel of Sarah's breast in his hand. He'd imagined this a thousand times but never in this setting.

His mouth was dry, and his dick was so hard, he wondered if his zipper would be permanently imprinted. Between the scent of her lip gloss and the feel of her on his thighs, he was already fighting for control.

He scraped his fingernail across her nipple, imitating what she'd done to him. She smiled at him, and her nipple hardened, so he assumed this was good. He trailed one hand across her breast, sliding underneath her arm, caressing the exposed skin down her arm. His other he slid around her waist pulling her closer.

She'd said he couldn't touch the skin unless it was exposed, but she'd worn one of her V-neck T-shirts. With her plump breasts, there was plenty of skin for him to taste, including the enticing valley between them. At the touch of his lips, she moaned and scooted closer.

Her skin held the smell of vanilla. He used to think it was from her cooking, but she had vanilla-scented lotion and vanilla-scented lip gloss. He was fascinated with how soft her breasts were and how much he enjoyed the sounds she was making.

Sarah had been hovering over his dick, and he'd wanted to feel her heat against him. When she moved even closer, she dropped her core down onto his dick. He tried to concentrate on tasting and nibbling her breasts, but Sarah hadn't stayed still when she dropped down.

She was grinding and making breathy moans while she did. He slid his hand up into her hair until she was facing him, so he could see her eyes.

"You said no completion. Does that include blowing in my jeans without skin exposed because that's where I think I'm heading. Between your scent, your taste, and your moans, I'm so close, and I've got that tingle that's telling me it won't take much. And I can feel the heat of your pussy through your jeans. Tell me, Sarah, what you want," his voice cracked at the end, and he didn't care. He was trying to calm his breathing, waiting on Sarah.

Her eyes were filled with need, and she didn't want to stop, but she had a plan. He wasn't getting carried away and screwing up her plan. If she wanted to make the plan, execute the plan, and then say fuck the plan, he was all for it, but she was running this show.

She closed her eyes for a second, then opened them as she lifted up a little. "Even though I want you more than anything, Scoop, I also want to give you all the experiences you missed. Thank you for stopping us."

Scoop leaned his head against the backrest, gazing at the top of the Bronco. He couldn't decide if he was the smartest man or the stupidest man tonight. He knew positively he was the most frustrated.

Chapter Nine

S arah sipped her coffee, waiting for Scoop to finish filling up the Bronco. She'd slept like a baby after their make-out session at the drive-in, but Scoop's attitude didn't seem like he had.

Most of their conversations were her asking a question and him grunting out a one-word reply. He reminded her a little right now of how David or Grant pouted when they didn't get a toy they wanted. Maybe he was irritated he hadn't been able to unwrap his toy last night. She probably shouldn't have played *Paradise by the Dashboard Light* as they left the theater last night. He'd rolled his eyes and laughed, but she'd known he'd been disgruntled since they hadn't gone farther, even though he was the one who ultimately stopped them.

She hid her smile as Scoop opened the door, then grabbed some wet wipes he kept in the vehicle. He wiped his hands, then got back out of the truck to throw the trash away.

She'd noticed he was fastidious about keeping his Bronco clean, and she couldn't blame him. It was a gorgeous vehicle he'd restored. He kept the windshield clean, and he'd washed the truck once already because he didn't want the bugs to stay stuck to the grill.

She actually liked that about him because she was the same way about her kitchen and her computer room, not so much the rest of her house. Each item had its place, and when she was finished, they were put back. Her bedroom was another story. She had a habit of trying on different items, then piling the clean clothes on a chair instead of hanging them back up. Remi, who was a neat freak too, couldn't understand how Sarah could be neat in a couple rooms and a complete disaster in others.

Sarah didn't know why and frankly, she didn't care. She was who she was and if people didn't like it, so be it. Scoop had gotten back in and gotten them on the road all without saying a word. She'd finished her coffee and was still craving something sweet. They'd eaten breakfast at the hotel, but she'd chosen some fruit and yogurt to get something healthy before they ate fast food today. Although a little sweet, it hadn't satisfied her craving. She reached into her candy bag and pulled out one of her suckers. Scoop glanced at her, then rolled his eyes.

"I will freaking buy you any other candy you want if you don't have any suckers today," he grumbled.

She stared at him, trying to figure out why he was being such an ass about her suckers. "Umm, why?"

"Please tell me Ms. Sex Ed teacher isn't that naïve. It was bad enough watching you suck on those things when we hadn't gotten close. After last night, every time your tongue wraps around that sucker, I imagine my dick's the sucker."

She bit her lip, holding back her smile, then decided to hell with it. She smiled, then snorted. After all her planning, who knew the suckers would break through his embarrassment. She giggled, then laughed.

"Is that why you're being an ass this morning?" she gasped out between laughs.

"I didn't sleep well last night, but if I'm being an ass, I'm sorry."

Scoop's words didn't match his tone. His voice screamed loud and clear he was in a pissy mood. Which honestly, she'd been wanting to re-create what he'd missed in high school, and she remembered a couple guys being assholes to her and her sisters after a date that didn't end up in putting out.

She worked to quit laughing, but every time she started to calm down, she'd think of him getting after her about the sucker and lose it again.

"I'm glad you're amused."

His tone wasn't quite so pissy, so maybe he was starting to see the humor.

"Well, we know you can't die from blue balls, so I'd say the experiment was a success."

She giggled, then reached for the sucker but stopped. Sucking on them was a habit. She wasn't giving them up, but she'd refrain from it today.

"I want chocolate at our next stop, and I'll leave the suckers alone for now."

"Done. If it's okay with you, I saw a Blazer for sale close to where we're going today. Would you be okay with a little side trip? It's not in great shape, but I need a new project."

She nodded. "I'm game. We loosely planned the trip so we could make changes along the way. We all took a turn learning about cars and motorcycles, so I enjoy seeing them."

Scoop's mouth turned up at her words. Seeing a different side to him this morning was good. She'd seen him irritated and frustrated multiple times when they had been chasing down leads about Bear and War's ex-chief and he'd seen her the same way. Today, they'd moved to a different place with their relationship–– their fake relationship. She had to remind herself about that. It was fake, and it would end when their trip was done.

She wondered if her heart would be intact when the trip was over. She'd agreed to the ground rules, but she hadn't realized how much it might change her. Everything she learned about Scoop made him more attractive. Giving up so much of his childhood to make sure his mom could get a better job and support them, and he could help so he and his siblings had the basic things they needed.

He'd had to be the man of the house before he ever had a chance to be a boy. If he didn't get to do any of the high school things most kids did, she wondered if he'd had fun at all. She loved the memories of racing her sisters on the dirt track close to their house. Being in a small town, they'd made their own fun.

She picked up her phone and looked for something they could do reminiscent of what she and her sisters experienced. She checked the surrounding towns of where they were staying the night and the towns along the way of their side trip.

She hid her smile because she wanted their activity to be a surprise for Scoop. The county fair near where they were looking at the Blazer had exactly what she was looking for. The town even had a couple of places with rooms still available. She reserved one for tonight and changed their hotel reservation to tomorrow night. Thank goodness she'd paid for the changeable reservations without any penalties.

Besides learning about sex, Scoop was going to experience some of the fun things she was betting his family didn't have the money for growing up.

SCOOP WALKED AROUND the 1973 Blazer which was in crappy shape. He'd known when the man didn't share pictures it would need a ton of work, but working on cars and motorcycles was one of his hobbies. It helped him relax after sitting at a desk in front of a computer all day.

Surprisingly, there wasn't a lot of rust. It was more body damage and general neglect over the years. The man had used it as a farm truck. The back of the vehicle had multiple tools to fix things on his property. The good thing was it ran, which, as far as Scoop was concerned, made the deal sweeter.

"So what are you thinking on a price?"

Scoop had liked the forthright manner of the man as soon as they stopped. He'd pointed out the issues with the vehicle instead of trying to gloss over them.

"Well, even with the engine running, I'd put it in fair condition or lower. She's got some body issues and none of my kids want her. I really want her to go to someone who will get her back to what she was or even better."

Scoop nodded, "She?"

"Yes, my late wife and I bought her together as our first new vehicle ever. Three thousand, seven hundred dollars plus tax. At the time, it was the largest purchase we'd ever made besides the farm. My wife named her Patricia."

Scoop waited for the man to give him a price. Everyone knew the person who waited to bargain had a little advantage. He worked to keep his emotions from not showing on his face because he felt like a kid in a candy store. He could already imagine what he wanted to do with the Blazer's interior, including replacing the carpet and seats. He'd need to check, but it looked like the dash might be salvageable.

"You seem like you'll take care of her. I can tell by your Bronco you'll take care of Patricia. How about fifteen thousand and you're good to go?"

Fifteen was higher than he wanted to pay with the body damage, but if he had to, he would.

"Is the Blazer the only thing for sale, or are you interested in unloading some of these motorcycle parts and motorcycles?" Sarah called from around the corner of the barn.

The farmer grinned. "Your girl sounds like she wants to spend some of your money. I'd be happy to sell my motorcycle stuff. Kids aren't interested in it, and between my arthritis in my hands and hip, I can't ride anymore, so no use restoring them."

Scoop followed the farmer around the side of the building. He glanced over to where Sarah was standing. Her eyes were dancing, but she wasn't grinning. Knowing Locks, each of his girls probably knew exactly how to bargain with a seller. Looking over the motorcycles, he walked over by Sarah. Sarah wasn't standing by the item which was worth the most. She was over by a couple of motorcycles that had seen better days. One was a Honda CB.

"What are you thinking, sweetheart?"

Scoop waited to see what Sarah would say because, depending on who was talking, she'd let them have it if she believed they were talking down to her.

"I'm thinking my dad would think I am the greatest daughter if I brought this Honda home for him. Which is saying a lot; I have four sisters, so I've got to work hard to be the favorite. Honestly, though, I'd be interested in taking the whole lot off your hands. My next to-youngest sister is our mechanic, and she's always looking for parts."

The farmer walked over to the pile of motorcycles and parts haphazardly leaned against the barn.

"Well, I could probably part with this stuff for around five thousand dollars."

Scoop couldn't believe he was offering Sarah everything for that. The 1970s Harley Davidson Ironhead Sportster was worth that. He didn't want to move anything, but he thought he could see another Harley underneath a layer of motorcycle parts.

"So, my daddy always told us girls to never accept the first offer, no matter what we thought of it. How about four thousand? I'll have to rent something to take it home in because I didn't plan on buying items this big."

"Well, if you can convince your man to pay the fifteen thousand for the Blazer and you pay five, I'll toss in that trailer as a bonus."

He waved toward a sixteen-foot enclosed trailer which looked like it had been used to transport racing cars. The Blazer would have no problem fitting in it, but adding the additional motorcycles and parts would send them over what his Bronco could tow.

He texted War to see who would be available to ride down and pull the trailer back. War said he could have two of the new guys, who were considering prospecting, there with a large enough truck to tow it back by later this afternoon.

"You've got a deal. I'll have to have someone else come and pick the items up later today. My Bronco won't tow that much weight."

"You all have a deal. Do you want to help load everything?"

Sarah nodded. "Yes. Do you have any of the titles for the bikes?"

"Let's head inside and we'll get our business taken care of and then work on loading."

Chapter Ten

Sarah smiled as they headed toward their bed-and-breakfast. She'd updated Scoop on their changed itinerary. He had been relieved because he wanted to stay and make sure the trailer was picked up.

He'd given the guys instructions twice to make sure they did exactly what he wanted. He'd even told them under no circumstances were they to open the trailer or get anything out of it. She'd appreciated him making sure she would be able to decide who she was giving the different motorcycle items to.

The hour drive to where they were staying would be the perfect time to tick another item off her list of Scoop's sex education. They'd both pulled drinks out of the cooler in the back. She was on her second bottle of water but didn't worry about having to stop. They were a little sweaty from loading all the items. Scoop had tried to tell her she didn't need to help. She wasn't missing uncovering all the cool motorcycles and parts she'd bought. There had been not one but three Harleys under the tarps plus all the parts, including a frame for an older Indian motorcycle. She hadn't explored enough to know more than that because they'd been on a time frame.

She had taken the time to appreciate Scoop's arms bulging as he lifted and moved items to the trailer. Watching him bend over in front of her multiple times had her thinking about seeing him nude in their room.

"Let's use the time driving to the hotel to accomplish one of the items on my list."

Scoop glanced over at her, cocking his eyebrow. Whether he was pushing his glasses up his nose or cocking his eyebrow at her, she had a hard time keeping her concentration on what they were supposed to be doing.

"What are you thinking we can accomplish while I'm driving? I don't want to be reckless."

"Seriously? You know me."

He nodded. "You're right. I know you're careful. So?"

"Let's start with how people talk to each other during sex. Did you read any of the books I gave you?"

"Yep." His tone was cracking her up. Right now, she was guessing she was his least favorite person.

"And?"

Scoop breathed deep and huffed out a breath. She could wait until he eventually talked. "It was hot."

"It is. I thought we'd practice to make it more comfortable. Plus, you only have to concentrate on words, not all the actions to go with it."

Scoop's face was already blushing and as much as she considered it adorable, they needed to get past this.

"Fine, I'll start. If you're nibbling on my breasts and touching them, I might say, please suck my nipples. Or I might say, Scoop, please taste me and hold my breast up to your mouth."

Scoop reached down to adjust his cock within his jeans before moving his hand back to the wheel and she bit her lips, hiding a smile.

"Fuck. Okay, do I have to describe what I'm doing or just say the fucking words?"

She chuckled. "You can just say the words. Just like dick, cock, penis, tally-wacker and so many other words describe a dick there are many words for breasts or a vagina. You have to pick the right one for the partner you're with."

Scoop shuddered, glanced at Sarah, then turned back to the road. His blush not only covered his cheeks, but his neck was red too.

"These are the prettiest breasts I've ever seen, and I can't wait to taste them again."

"Oh, that was good. Would it be easier if we took turns?"

Scoop rolled his eyes, and she covered her mouth with her hand. She hadn't realized how much she'd enjoy teasing him while she taught him.

"Nothing about this is easy but yeah, turns would be fucking great."

"I want to taste and lick every inch of your cock."

Scoop shuddered, and she questioned if they should go on, but if he was having trouble concentrating on driving, he'd tell her.

"Your pussy is so pretty, and I can't wait to lick and feast on you for hours."

Sarah swallowed and realized Scoop wasn't the only one affected. Imagining him licking and sucking on her pussy had her squirming in her seat for relief. Time to up the heat.

"Put that big dick in my pussy and fuck me hard, Scoop."

"I can't wait until I'm deep inside your pussy and you're clamping me tight as I make you come until you scream my name."

Sarah flicked the air conditioner a little cooler and turned up the fan. It didn't matter what the outside temperature was. Scoop's words were turning her on.

Her turn, but his words had stunned her and knocked every thought out of her head except having him act out his words. Imagining him inside her, pounding away until she screamed, had her nipples pebbling. Never had anyone made her so crazy she screamed their name.

She might have to cut this little experiment short, but she also wanted to have the same effect on Scoop he was having on her.

"I want you to grab my hair and plunge your cock inside my mouth. I'll lick every inch of your shaft and balls until you're trembling and can't help spilling into my mouth and down my throat."

Scoop readjusted again, then tapped the steering wheel as he drove.

"I want to take all your clothes off, uncovering each hidden treasure. After I nibble and taste each inch of your body, I'm going to lay down. You'll crawl up my body until your knees are on each side of my face. You'll lower your perfect little pussy down until I can taste every sweet inch of her until you shake and shiver with your release."

Game over. Scoop had won. Heck, she almost had a mini orgasm from his words alone.

"Oh look, there's the turnoff to the town." Sarah fanned her face as she leaned back. *Note to self: Scoop was a fast learner and had no problem once he got started talking dirty.* She worked to calm herself down. She wanted a quick shower before they went to the fair. No, she really wanted to jump over all the steps and have Scoop do exactly what he'd described to her, but if she only had less than two weeks, she wasn't skipping a step. She was going to enjoy and savor each one.

Chapter Eleven

Scoop bought the tickets and then slid his arm around Sarah's waist. They'd checked in and showered in record time. He hadn't wanted to chance staying in the room longer than necessary. After their dirty talk in the truck, he'd been consumed by thoughts of having Sarah. His problem was he wasn't confident enough to initiate anything. Although he'd been learning things, he still felt completely out of his depth.

He'd missed a lot in high school and college. Talking with girls. Learning what they liked with kissing and touching. He didn't regret what he'd done because he loved Rose and Tasha. He wished he had more confidence with women. No, with Sarah.

Once he'd seen her at the clubhouse, all the other women had faded away. He was attracted to her, but it was more than that. He enjoyed being in her company. The road trip with her had been a blast. Sharing the sights with her had made everything special.

"Where to?"

Sarah had on jeans, tennis shoes and a long-sleeved T-shirt. She'd pulled her hair back and braided it.

"First, we're going to do an experience I'm guessing you didn't have in high school and then we'll wander the carnival part of the fair."

She wanted to do an experience out here in the open at the carnival? Did he hear her right?

She started giggling, then chuckling. "Oh my gosh, your face. Not one of those experiences. C'mon. I'll show you."

She grasped his hand, tugging him along. Letting Sarah lead him gave him a fantastic view of her curvy butt which was not what he needed right now. His jeans were tight enough without his dick trying to punch through the zipper.

He tried to think about what experience she could be thinking of. As they made their way through the crowded area, Sarah led him toward a temporary fence that had been erected. The inside of the fence had hay bales stacked inside it.

"Go-karts?" he questioned.

"Yep, have you raced before, Mint Chocolate Chip?"

He chuckled, grinning at her. "No, but I have to tell you, I'm a whiz at Mario Kart. I came in second in the clubhouse championship."

"You guys had a Mario Kart tournament?"

"We've had a Mario Kart tournament, a Call of Duty tournament, ping-pong, pool and so many others. If it can be bet on, we do it."

"I'm a little miffed that you guys have been there this long and never invited any of us to participate. I think I'm going to kick your butt today and enjoy doing it."

"You're on. Winner picks what we eat for supper?" Scoop waited while Sarah contemplated his request. She liked her food and probably had already scoped out what carnival items she wanted to try.

"Deal." Sarah held her hand out to shake. He shook her hand, fighting the impulse to pull her closer and kiss her. Kissing her was the only thing he was confident he could do well. Besides Sarah's reactions when he kissed her, she'd been vocal about his kisses, making her forget what they were supposed to be doing.

"Just know, Rocky Road, I want to win by my skill, not because you threw the race."

"Prepare to lose then."

He handed the tickets over, and they made their way to the go-karts. They were handed helmets and given instructions. He got in his car and waited for Sarah. She followed the hand motions of their instructor and took her place at the starting line.

It wasn't long before they had the spots filled to start the race. He watched the stoplight to the side and when it flicked green, he took his foot off the brake and pressed the gas to the floor. Besides being a competitive guy, he didn't want to deal with the fallout of losing to Sarah. He'd never hear the end of it once they were back at the clubhouse.

He wasn't sure how many times they were supposed to go around the track, but on the first turn, Sarah took the lead. She went high, which should have meant she'd be slower, but she moved into second. Scoop stayed right behind her but couldn't find a way to pass.

He stayed close thinking as they passed their first lap around the track, he'd go high like she did. Once again, Sarah went high and then passed the cart in first place. He couldn't figure out how it was working. They passed the lap mark, and the white flag was out, indicating it was their last lap.

He could not believe how good she was. On turn three, he passed the guy in second and moved in behind Sarah. They had one turn left then the straightaway to the finish. He stayed close, but he also didn't want to bump her. With a dirt track, it wouldn't be hard to accidentally send her into the edge of the track lined with hay bales.

They completed the last turn and as they moved to the straightaway, he tried to move even with Sarah. Despite having his foot to the floor, his front tires were coming along her back, but he couldn't pull even. As they crossed the finish line and the checkered flag waved, Sarah beat him by at least half a go-kart length. He slowed down, driving around the track to where the staff motioned them to stop.

He unbuckled and pulled his helmet off to Sarah's cheering. "Woohoo! Looks like we're having cotton candy, pretzels, and funnel cakes for supper tonight."

Her smile lit her whole face and even with a smudge of dirt from the dust of the track, she was gorgeous.

"Congratulations, Mario Andretti. Do you want to play any games or ride anything before we gorge ourselves on carnival food?"

He reached for her hand as they exited the track, finally giving in to kissing her lips. He didn't care who saw them. She was captivating and he couldn't stop himself.

Sarah's lips clung to his, and the faint taste of salt from her sweat didn't detract at all.

"Let's try a couple of games, Fudge Ripple, then supper. We'll see who can win one of those big stuffed animals at the shooting game."

She laughed and danced ahead of him, holding her hands up, shaking her fingers in the air, and chanting 'I'm number one.' Giving her up at the end of the trip if he couldn't convince her to take a chance on him for real was going to suck.

Chapter Twelve

S coop made sure they'd packed everything, then used the spray and paper towels he carried in his Bronco to clean the windshield and mirrors. Sarah had found an outdoor flea market in Liberty Falls.

Yesterday, even though Sarah was vocal that she didn't like to sweat or exercise besides what her job required, they hiked to Turner Falls. He'd found good parking, so it was only about a ten-minute walk. They'd taken pictures of the falls and then another visitor had offered to take their picture with the falls as backdrop. He'd had her use his phone because he wanted that picture.

Someone else looking at their smiles would never guess they were fake dating, but it didn't feel fake to him. Every experience, every touch, and every deep thought they shared pulled him deeper in until he couldn't imagine not getting to spend time with her.

He stashed the cleaner and roll of paper towels in his toolbox. He hoped they'd have enough room for everything they seemed to be picking up along the way. He was looking forward to the flea market today and holding Sarah's hand as they browsed the booths. Her eyes would light up when she spotted something.

He enjoyed just being around her, spending time together. Her views on family were in line with his own. She'd do anything for the ones that were hers by blood and those who'd become family along the way. Family was everything to her, and it was to him too.

He'd have their back just like they'd have his. Hard times happened, but with family, they'd help you up when you couldn't see a way forward.

When War and Bear had talked about the Bluff Creek Brotherhood MC, Scoop had known he would leave the job and follow them when they left. He'd been so tired of trying to make a difference but failing at every turn due to all the corruption in their department.

From the first moment he'd set foot on the property and Regina had welcomed him, a peace had settled over him. Until it did, he'd had no idea how stressed he'd been. His job with the MC was still stressful but in a different way. He didn't want to let anyone down by not keeping them safe. He worked security and tech, but he was also the secretary of the club. Compass who'd been the original secretary had done a quick two-week course on being the secretary and then gone nomad.

Scoop would have floundered, and Regina might be classified as Baron's Ol' Lady, but she had a firm grasp on most of the positions in the MC. With her business acumen, Compass had relied on Regina a lot in the last couple of years after he lost his wife. Scoop was thankful for that because when Compass went nomad, he quit answering Scoop's calls. Regina had ended up answering his questions.

He settled into the seat, taking his cup of coffee from Sarah. "You ready for this? Besides Fiestaware, are we searching for anything else?"

Sarah leaned over, touching his cheek. "Nope, just a fun day of shopping at a flea market and then maybe a lesson tonight."

Her eyes twinkled, and he knew she'd done it on purpose. Her eyes glanced down to his lap, then she smiled because she saw exactly what she'd done to him. Her lips came closer, then she was claiming his mouth, and he reveled in getting to taste her. Time fell away when she was close. Her taste, with a faint hint of the cream in her coffee, was one of his favorite flavors. Right up there with the grape or strawberry Tootsie Pop suckers she favored.

Her fingers slid across his jaw as she pulled away. She settled back in her seat, slipping the seatbelt over her, the belt bisecting her breasts and wrapping around her waist. He was freaking thirty-five and wanting to be the belt so he could wrap himself around her. At least they had about a twenty-minute drive so he could get his dick to deflate a little.

Maybe if he concentrated on her family, it would go down a little faster.

"How's the construction coming along? Did they send any more pictures?"

"No. Construction is on track, but they won't be uploading any more pictures because Dad said it wasn't secure."

Scoop chuckled. "Your dad told you that the site you set up wasn't secure? So what did you say to him?"

Even though Locks loved and appreciated all his daughters' skills, Scoop had noticed there were still times when he would tell them his opinion as if it was fact.

"I decided I was having too good of a trip to argue. Plus, Jesse said she'd upload them for me later."

He loved how the sisters listened to their dad, but if they didn't agree, they just did whatever they wanted without him knowing. It seemed to work well for them.

"I think that's a perfect response."

Sarah nodded. "Yep. Remi said he's been cranky, so I'm cutting him a little slack. She thinks it has to do with Mom not being here to see the grandkids."

Scoop flicked the blinker on, turning and following the signs to the parking. He'd thought it was all outside, but the signs indicated their destination was a large building. He grabbed his stuff and walked around to open Sarah's door.

Her V-neck T-shirt was white. She had on one of the pairs of jeans that, if he hadn't seen her slide them on, he would be positive they were painted on. A white and orange plaid shirt was tied around her waist. After sliding her purse over her shoulder and across her body, she grasped his hand as he helped her out of the truck.

"Do we need the wagon?"

Sarah had brought a collapsible wagon for them to use for the big flea markets and the author signing event.

"Let's leave it. Parking is close and who knows if we'll find anything."

He closed the door and beeped the lock and alarm. He started to take Sarah's hand again, but she lifted his arm and snuggled under it, wrapping her arm around his waist. He slid his arm around her shoulder and walked toward the building. Nine days left to be the fake boyfriend and convince her she couldn't live without him or go back to being just friends and try to pick up the pieces of his heart.

Chapter Thirteen

Sarah was standing near the dresser with Scoop standing behind her. She'd had the perfect day shopping, but her thoughts had been consumed with her plans for tonight. Her stomach was churning, and her heart was racing. She was petrified to teach him but was going to push through. Scoop deserved her best.

His arm was wrapped around her. Her back flush against his chest. She directed him to pay special attention to zones one through six, then undress her, and he could touch zones seven through eleven at his own pace.

She was watching his reflection as they stood in front of the mirror. His warm breath then lips against her neck had her shivering.

Today they'd laughed, joked, and talked. She never ran out of things to talk with him about, and she wanted to pretend their relationship wasn't fake. She wanted to watch Scoop push his glasses up his nose when he was concentrating or run his hands through his hair when he was frustrated.

She wanted the right to run her hands all over his body, especially his arms, with the dusting of hair and hard biceps. Despite sitting in front of a computer, Scoop's body was perfect, in her opinion.

Scoop's hand slid the straps of her camisole off her shoulders. "I must be failing this part if you're thinking about other things."

She looked into his eyes in the mirror. Scoop's heated as he uncovered her breasts and lifted his hands to cup them.

"Maybe I need to add the dirty talk into this to make sure you stay in the moment."

"I'm sorry. I was just overthinking."

His hands massaged her breasts, then he caught her nipples between his thumbs and forefingers, tugging the peaks until they were hard.

"I love feeling these gorgeous girls. You're curvy and the hint of skin that peeks out through your V-neck has me imagining sucking them all day."

Scoop's words heated her core, and she wanted to relax and just enjoy the moment, but that wasn't what this was about.

"What else do you like?" Sarah asked as Scoop pushed the camisole over her generous hips, leaving her in her lacy underwear. Playing with one breast, he skimmed his other hand down her stomach, his touch leaving a tingle in its wake.

"I love the way your skin feels against my fingers. The look of your lighter-colored skin against my tan hands. The smell of your scent filling my nostrils until it's all I can smell."

Tonight wasn't about going all the way, but it sure felt like it. Looking in the mirror, she didn't recognize the wanton woman in the mirror. She'd become someone else with Scoop. She wasn't trying to be the perfect date, the perfect woman for once.

She was teaching him, but she was learning, too. "Let's move to the bed and you get to experience zones twelve through seventeen. But we're not having sex, or I should say we're not having penetration with your cock. You're going to satisfy me with your fingers and mouth, and I'm going to do the same for you."

Scoop noticeably swallowed, and his blush reddened his cheeks. "Okay," he squeaked out.

She walked to the bed, holding her hand out for Scoop. His warm fingers grasped hers, and he stared into her eyes. "Slide my panties off."

He breathed deep, then reached toward her hips, tugging one side down. When the other side caught on her butt, his brow furrowed. She wasn't helping on this part. He was smart. He'd figure out that with her full figure, he'd need both hands.

He tugged her hand up and placed it on his shoulder as he bent down, tucking his index fingers into her panties, then tugging them down until they passed her thighs. They fell to the floor and his face was near her belly button. She waited to see if he'd do something or if he needed a nudge.

He stood up, scooted closer and slid his arms around her, grasping her butt cheeks and lifting her up. "Do you want to be lying on the bed or sitting on it, Ms. Franks?"

"Lying in the middle."

He gently placed her in the middle of the bed and laid down beside her. She could do this. She'd teach him all he needed to know and not let her heart become involved. It was just sex, right?

SCOOP LAID BESIDE SARAH, mesmerized by her skin. She was everything and more than he imagined. His dick was hard, and he heartily hoped he didn't embarrass himself when he tried to satisfy her. Her scent was intoxicating. He imagined her pussy would smell even better.

He reached out and slid his finger across her stomach, then a little farther to where her blonde hair covered her mound. She didn't shave it all, thank goodness, but had a neatly trimmed area. Her legs were together, and he wondered if it was okay to slide his hand down to open them.

"So once the clothes are off, most people go straight to the genitals. It's all about the cock and pussy, but there's so much more." Her finger brushed Scoop's abs but bypassed his cock to slide down his leg. "There's the back of the knee." Her fingers brushed behind his knee and a shiver worked its way down his spine.

"Your dick looks pretty hard, red and angry. How about I satisfy you first so you might have a chance of listening to my instructions?"

Scoop nodded because suddenly his mouth was so freaking dry, he wasn't sure he could squeak out an answer.

Sarah's hand wandered up from his knee, sliding between his legs, her hand caressing his thigh. "The inside of the thigh is sensitive for fingers or a mouth." She followed her words by leaning over, nibbling, and kissing from his knee up his thigh.

"Oh fuck!" Scoop groaned. At this rate, he was going to come before she got her mouth on him.

Her hand slid closer, her fingers ruffling through the hair at the base of his cock. "I like that you have this trimmed back a little. So just like I have a huge amount of nerve endings plus a clitoris, you have some special places too. I want you to try to hold back and not come until I say yes, but if you can't, that's okay."

Her smile was a little devious, and he wondered if she was going to try to make him lose control. What she didn't realize is with her, he didn't have any control. He was hoping the first touch of her mouth didn't have him blowing immediately.

"Like here," Sarah's hand wrapped around his shaft while her tongue licked around the head, paying special attention to the V underneath. The feel of her tongue and hand had him thrusting up toward her involuntarily. She licked down his shaft, following one of the veins until she sucked a ball into her mouth while caressing the other.

He'd been completing missing out by giving his shaft some rough tugs. Sarah made it infinitely better. She continued playing, and he focused on tightening his toes and his abs to hold back. His spine tingled as Sarah licked around his head again.

"Come whenever you want," she whispered, then put her mouth on his dick, engulfing it down to her hand. His shaft hit the back of her throat and the warm, wet feeling of her mouth had him grasping her head with his hands and coming. His heart raced and the rush of release felt like fireworks.

When he was able to think again, Sarah was licking his release off his cock with a grin on her face.

"How was that?"

"Spectacular. Orgasmic. The best thing I've ever felt." His hand cupped her face. His heart felt like he was where he was supposed to always be. How the fuck was he going to get through this? She didn't care he'd come immediately. In fact, she'd encouraged it. Having her mouth on him made him realize he couldn't picture being with anyone else. Not having sex or even dating. In a short five days, the fascination he'd had with Sarah had grown into love and it wasn't all because she was teaching him about sex. It was everything about her. Her love for her job, her family, and the way she was nurturing. When she walked into the room, his heart warmed.

"Now it's your turn. Let me lay you down."

Sarah giggled and shook her head. "I want to lie on your shoulder and go to sleep."

"That's not what you said earlier. You said you wanted me to learn how to make you come with my mouth and fingers."

Sarah blushed and shook her head. "It was so hot while I was sucking you off that I rubbed my clit and came when you did. Tonight is perfect just like this. Tomorrow, we'll have you satisfy me. Now lie down and let me snuggle against your shoulder."

He nodded and held his arm out for her. Something was different, but he couldn't tell what. He didn't understand why Sarah had changed the plan. For now, he'd cuddle her and go to sleep.

Chapter Fourteen

S arah was debating a nap while Scoop drove. They'd stopped at a couple of outdoor flea markets and walked a lot. They'd stayed up late last night watching a movie and messing around, and she was dragging today.

They had a couple more hours before they reached where they were staying tonight. They had a couple activities near the hotel they'd talked about but hadn't decided on.

Her watch went off with a Code Ross followed by a text requesting Sarah immediately download the footage from inside the range and the outdoor cameras from fifteen minutes ago to current. Copies to be sent to Beth, Jesse, and Ellie.

"Code Ross. Isn't that everything's not alright and help is needed?"

Sarah grabbed her computer and opened it up. "Yes. I need a strong signal, so can you exit at the gas station?"

Scoop flicked his blinker on and exited. Sarah waited for her computer to boot up.

When Scoop pulled over and parked, Sarah brought out her mobile hotspot and pulled up the footage from the range. She could have done it on the road, but the mobile hotspot worked a little better if they were sitting in place. She went back fifteen minutes, then watched to make sure she had what they were talking about. She didn't see anyone breaking into the range, so she continued scanning until she saw a body and paused.

Was that Flick running around the range with only his boots on? Where the heck were the rest of his clothes and wasn't that freaking uncomfortable having his dick bounce? Then Cannon, the two guys who picked up the Blazer, and Roam came running around the building.

Scoop leaned over her shoulder. "What the hell is happening while we're away?"

"I don't know." Sarah watched the rest of the footage showing the guys going back into the range and chatting but not getting dressed. Then the door opened, and Beth, Jesse, and Ellie walked in. The guys immediately put their hands down to cover themselves, and Cannon directed them to leave.

Beth shook her head no, then leaned over the counter and grabbed the computer that the range used to monitor the cameras. They ran out of the range, jumping in the car with Cannon chasing them while they drove away.

Sarah copied the video and sent it to Ellie and all her sisters, then sent one to her special place.

"Hey, you're not going to give them a copy, are you?"

Scoop's voice was a little irate. She'd always have her sisters' backs unless it conflicted with her man. This didn't conflict at all.

"Of course I am. Why wouldn't I?"

"Well, because Cannon didn't want them to have it."

"He may not have wanted them to, but he, as well as all the guys, know we have video surveillance all over that place. If they didn't want video, they could have turned off the cameras. They streaked all around the range during the day. If they're going to be stupid, then they can live with the consequences."

Sarah waited while Scoop stared at her. She knew him. He was thinking through all the options. He looked at her and nodded.

"My first inclination was to protect them because that's what I always do and if they had contacted me first, I would have deleted the footage for them. However, they didn't contact me at all and you're right. Cannon, Roam and Flick all know about the cameras and chose to not shut them off. I do want to know why they decided to do it. Can you go back before they streaked and see if we can hear their conversation?"

Sarah laughed and looked for the footage.

SCOOP FILLED THE VEHICLE with gas while Sarah ran inside to the bathroom. He wasn't low enough to need gas, but Sarah had drunk two bottles of water and wanted to stop.

He couldn't stop laughing about why the guys had streaked. Roam basically calling them all babies and saying they weren't acting like a real MC had been what had prompted them to all streak. How those guys had thought streaking would be acting like a real MC was beyond him. Why didn't they take a bike ride or plan the poker run they had coming up?

Scoop hadn't gotten to know Roam as well as he knew War. Roam had returned to Bluff Creek after the Army and joined Rascal at Bluff Creek Ink. Roam lived with his parents to have help with his kids and most of the time when Scoop saw him, if he wasn't with his kids, he was sitting at the bar in the clubhouse drinking.

Scoop wasn't going to judge because he wasn't in Roam's shoes. His kids' mom just decided one day she didn't want to be a mom. Working at the police department had given him firsthand knowledge that some men and women shouldn't be allowed to procreate. Some people didn't deserve kids.

He was glad she'd left the kids with Roam because he couldn't imagine the life they would have had. With the MC, they had their grandparents but also so many uncles and aunts. They were one big family.

He finished gassing up and then cleaned the windshield. He pulled up to the front of the gas station to wait for Sarah. There were people waiting in line for the pumps.

His phone rang, and he worked to keep the laughter from his voice as he answered Roam's call.

"Hey, what's up?"

"Don't act like you don't know what I need your help with. I'm sure those women have already talked with Sarah. I need that footage deleted."

Roam was smart and a fantastic tattoo artist, but Scoop wasn't positive Roam grasped what had already happened with the footage.

"I'm happy to delete it from where we store it."

"Great. I really don't want everyone watching us all act like dumbasses."

"I said I could delete it from where we store it. It's already been copied and given to numerous people. I can't do anything about that."

"What the hell, Scoop!?"

"Can I ask why you all didn't turn off the video before you did it?"

He couldn't care less if they streaked or did anything else, but why the hell hadn't anyone turned off the cameras? The back room had a place to oversee the whole area.

"Flick said he'd turned it off, but I guess he just turned off the screens in the room."

Roam's disgruntled voice had Scoop glad they weren't doing a video call.

"Sorry I couldn't help. How's everything else going?"

"The diner is doing phenomenal and with Bear and Regina marketing to bikers, Rascal and I are overbooked, even adding extra evening hours at the tattoo shop. I think we'll need to add another artist soon."

"Not a bad problem to have, but I'm sure it's hard not being around your kids as much."

"Yes. Plus, Rascal would rather cut his hours anyway. He, Locks, and Baron want to spend more time with the grands which is great but leaves a lot on me. Enough about me. How's the trip? You swept her off her feet yet?"

"It's a great trip. We're getting to know each other, but I don't know how to show her I want her for more than the trip."

Scoop stared out the windshield, watching Sarah shop in the store, then head to the checkout. Her hair was in a ponytail he wanted to slide his fingers through and pull out. He loved her hair blowing around them as he kissed her.

"Well, I'm not an expert because I've never been in love with a woman, but I know I would have loved if my wife put me or the kids first. Think about how you can make everything easier for her. Gotta go. I've got a client in ten minutes."

Roam was gone before he could respond. This love stuff wasn't easy, especially when he was pretending they were in a fake relationship. Making things easier on her and putting her first. Maybe he could get her stuff at the signing. He'd do a little research tonight on who her favorite authors were and see if they had some special stuff available.

Chapter Fifteen

S coop walked behind Sarah, pulling her cart and taking pictures as she met the authors she had on her list. He'd scoped out her list and contacted a couple of the authors. He'd explained what he wanted for her. If she had preorders, he checked if there was anything special they had that he could add. He knew they only brought limited stock to signings because of space.

Jesse and Winnie had been more than happy to induct him into the world of book signings. His first surprise for her was with the author Sarah was getting ready to talk with. He hoped she loved it and he hadn't overstepped.

"Oh, I'm sorry. I only had one preorder."

The author smiled and then said, "Your man contacted me. He bought you some extras I had on hand."

The author pulled out one of the shirts he'd bought her. He'd thought it suited her perfectly.

I'm not addicted to reading. You're just not interesting enough to keep my attention.

She turned around and looked at him. He walked forward, sliding an arm around her shoulders.

"I want this to be memorable, so I decided you needed a couple extra treats. Now, let's get a picture with you two."

Sarah nodded and stood by one of her favorite authors and smiled one of the widest smiles he'd seen her with. Yep, he did good with his surprise.

He had four more planned, so by the time they left, she'd have enough souvenirs of their day. Tonight, they were staying at a hotel near the edge of town. They were getting an early start to head back through Texas.

Last night, they'd done nothing. By the time they grabbed food to take to the hotel, they'd checked in, eaten, and taken showers. When he got out of his shower, Sarah had been deeply asleep. He'd actually been thankful because there wasn't any way he could have performed anything last night. He'd assumed he was in shape, but the time in the car and the walking they'd done had him aching. He'd popped some pain relievers and crawled into bed. He'd laughed because Sarah talked about how she did the minimum amount of running to stay in shape for work, but she loved hiking. If things turned out the way he wanted, he could see them hiking all fifty states.

He followed Sarah to the next author. She was wearing one of her flowy skirts with a V-neck blouse. Each piece cupped her assets, and he was having a hard time not spending the whole signing hard as a rock. She'd added her cowboy boots since they weren't hiking today and some silver bracelets which jingled as she walked.

When Sarah stopped, he got the camera ready because this was one of the big presents he'd gotten her. He'd texted her sisters to make sure he wasn't duplicating because he'd bought her the author's whole backlist of paperbacks, a couple totes, and more T-shirts.

"Hi, I'm so excited to meet you. I have a preorder: Sarah Franks."

The author giggled and motioned to her assistant. "I think we need to have my assistant take a pic of us."

The assistant picked up two full tote bags, setting them on the table.

"I only ordered three books," Sarah said.

"Yes, but someone else bought you all the other books in my backlist and some other goodies. Plus, his order was my largest, so I added a tumbler and a couple other swag items. My assistant can take a picture with you, your generous benefactor, and me, if that works."

Sarah turned to him with glistening eyes, biting her lip. "You so shouldn't have, but I love it." She threw her arms around him and hugged him. Her breasts rubbing against him and her scent wrapping around him had him giving up trying not to get hard. Hopefully, the picture would be from the waist up, or maybe he'd scoot behind Sarah to hide it.

Scoop smiled at Sarah and kissed her nose. He'd had no idea how much fun giving her presents would be, but right now, he wanted to spend the rest of his life giving her everything she'd ever dreamed of. The joy on her face was addicting. "Now, let's get your picture."

He stood for the picture, then followed her to the next author. Honestly, the book signing was fun to be at, but it gave him entirely too much time to think about tonight. He wondered if he should rub one out in the shower so he didn't pop off as soon as he got inside her.

If the last couple days had taught him anything, it was that he was head over heels for Sarah Franks. He'd thought he'd wanted forever before he asked her to help him, but being together each day had cemented that in his mind and his heart.

Sarah Franks was the woman for him, and he wanted to make their first time together perfect because if he had anything to do with it, it would be her last first time with anyone.

He'd scoped out a country bar to take her to dinner, then dancing, and then he hoped she'd be teaching him to rock her world.

SARAH SMILED SO MUCH her cheeks were hurting. She'd known she'd love getting to see a lot of her favorite authors today, but Mint Chocolate Chip had outdone her wildest dreams. The books, T-shirts, and extra goodies were wonderful, but his attitude as she meandered to all the authors was a gift, too. He didn't rush her. He also asked her opinion and then purchased some books for his mom and sisters.

She was anticipating tonight with Scoop. Dinner, dancing, and introducing him to sex. Heck, just thinking about it, and him, had her panties damp. Scoop was one gorgeous specimen of a man. Seeing him each night in his pajama pants had her ready to unwrap each delicious inch of him.

Her phone vibrated. It was probably her sisters.

Beth: How's the book signing?

Jesse: How's the sex?

Remington: Have you taught him how to find a clit and exactly what to do with it? Does he have any piercings?

Beth: Are you ignoring us?

Jesse: Are you having fun?

Remington: I want to go to a book signing. Is there another one we could all go to?

Beth: I think you're ignoring us. COME ON. I have to live vicariously through you because it's been a long, dry spell. Was it spectacular?

Winnie: Sorry. Phoebe and David decided to help me by changing Joey's poopy diaper.

Beth: Oh shit.

Jesse: Do you need help?

Winnie: He was in his bed. They just pulled off his diaper and got another out. He wasn't finished.

Beth: Ewwww.

Remington: Oh yuck. I'm super sorry I'm in Dodge City on a job.

Winnie: Liar. Rascal and Dad were here. They cleaned Phoebe and David. I took care of Joey.

Remington: Why did Phoebe and David need cleaned?

Winnie: They dropped the diaper on the floor then accidentally stepped in it and got it all over their hands while they tried to clean it up. Then the dogs decided to help and grabbed the diaper and ran.

Jesse: Is it bad I'm laughing so hard tears are running down my face? I'm never having kids. Too messy.

Sarah: It's great. We haven't yet. Tonight's the night. Love you and sorry about the poopapalooza. Gotta get back to the signing.

She texted them, giggling as she put her phone back in her bag.

"What's so funny?" Scoop whispered close to her ear. His warm breath sending shivers down her spine.

"Winnie's dealing with poopapalooza. The kids decided to help change Joey and got poop everywhere, plus Joey wasn't finished when they removed his diaper. Then the dogs grabbed the diaper too."

Scoop chuckled, "Those kids are hysterical. I bet even though it was disgusting, Winnie is glad to see Phoebe and David feeling at home. Any more authors, or are you ready to go?"

Sarah leaned up and kissed Scoop's cheek. "Yeah, I think she's not seeing the positive of that yet. Yes, I'm ready, and thank you for a perfect day."

He nodded and slid his hand to the back of her waist, pulling her cart and guiding her toward the exit. She was nervous about tonight but feeling the warmth of his hand through her clothes had her wanting more. His hands sliding across her skin and his lips touching her. She only hoped her instructions lived up to his expectations.

Chapter Sixteen

S coop finished his last bite of steak and wiped his mouth. Sarah had finished her chicken and was swaying her shoulders to the music. She had dancing on her itinerary as something she wanted to do. He wanted to feel her in his arms, but the majority of what they were playing was country. He'd never danced to country, so Sarah might need to do a little more teaching tonight for him.

"Would you like to dance?"

Sarah grinned and nodded. She started to stand, and he put a hand up to have her wait.

"So I've never actually country danced. I'm guessing they're two-stepping?"

"Yes, it's not hard. It's two quicks and two slows and your left hand holds my right up and your other hand is on my shoulder blade. Mine will be on your shoulder."

"I think I understand. I guess we can try."

He thought he got it, but he was a visual learner, so he'd just have to get out there and try. Sarah pulled her phone out and typed in something. Then she turned toward him.

"Rocky Road, I've worked with you long enough to know this might help."

She held up an instructional video of the two-step and pressed play. He watched the dance coach and partner explain the dance. He smiled and then held his hand out to Sarah. He so got this. Her hand felt warm and soft as he intertwined their fingers. They found a spot on the dance floor, and he slid his hand to her shoulder blade and held up his left hand. The smile he adored flashed across her face, and she cocked her eyebrow, waiting for him to lead them. He nodded at the woman that had entranced him and took the first steps to Diamond Rio's *Meet in the Middle*. Sarah had listened to this song on repeat when it was her turn for the music.

He concentrated on the steps, dancing her around the floor. Once they'd gone a couple times around the floor, he gained some confidence and spun her around, then back to him like the dance instructor had done. Sarah had a glow about her as they danced. Most of the time when they were researching, she had an intent look, but their time together had been special and relaxed both of them.

He thought back to the first time he'd seen her. He'd been eating Sunday lunch at the MC, and he couldn't take his eyes off her. When her sister had asked his name, Sarah had immediately asked him if it was like the ice cream. Since then, she'd called him the different ice cream names, and even though his brothers teased him about it, secretly he loved it. He had his own secret name for her, but he hadn't said it out loud.

Saying it out loud made it real, and he was worried if all they had was this one trip, would he be able to put his heart back together? It was getting harder and harder to not accidentally call her it.

The music switched to a slower number with John Michael Montgomery's *I Swear*, another of Sarah's favorites. She stepped closer, sliding her hands up around his neck and when he hesitated, she moved his hands to her waist. The other couples around them were slow dancing close together, most of them just swaying. He could do this, but there was no way she wouldn't feel how his body reacted to her. Her breasts pressed against him, and her head lay a little below his shoulder. He placed a kiss on top of her hair. He wasn't sure if that was a friend thing to do or a boyfriend thing. He was feeling so much more than friends, but he still had to play the part of the fake boyfriend. His cock hardened with her so close, and every move of their bodies had Sarah's light scent filling the air.

"Scoop?"

Her whisper of his name had the hairs on his arm raising and every nerve is his body on edge.

"Yes?" he croaked.

"Let's go back to the hotel. I think it's time we did another hands-on lesson."

Oh, fuck, fuck, fuck. Her words. Her scent. He only hoped she didn't touch him in the truck because he'd most likely embarrass himself. Maybe if he concentrated on running code, he could stay in control.

He nodded and followed her off the dance floor. He wasn't sure how he'd handle seeing her completely unclothed again. He'd seen a lot, but her lush breasts in his hands would probably have him losing it. Seeing her juicy ass moving underneath her skirt didn't help him stay in control.

SARAH FINISHED DRYING her hair. She had to admit she was procrastinating. She wanted Scoop with every fiber of her being, but the weight she carried worrying if she screwed up was overwhelming.

"Hey, you know, I'm good if you aren't feeling it tonight." Scoop's voice, through the door, drifted to a mutter. She couldn't understand his last sentence.

She took a deep breath, smiled, and opened the door. "I heard, *if you aren't feeling it tonight* but couldn't hear what you said after that."

Scoop closed his eyes, and a blush spread across his cheeks, and yes, her eyes tracked the blush as it continued down his neck onto his chest. "I just smarted off."

Sarah slid her fingers onto Scoop's chest, gliding back and forth, brushing his nipple on each pass. "I'm sure. That's why I wanted to hear it."

He opened his eyes, and she truly understood what the phrase: *his eyes blazed with heat* meant in her novels. The look in his eyes had her body coming to life, ready for anything with Scoop. She clenched her thighs as the fierce ache to have him swamped her. Each day, growing closer to him physically and emotionally, had her fighting to keep her head in instructor mode. Fake boyfriend. Fake relationship. She was his tutor in all things about women but not his girlfriend.

"I said I likely won't die if I don't feel the clasp of your pussy, even though it might seem like it."

Sarah giggled at Scoop's beleaguered tone. She stepped closer until their bodies were brushing each other, and she could feel the heat coming off him.

"Well, we can't have that, Rocky Road."

Her hands slid up and clasped around his neck. "How about we start off with you giving me a kiss? I want you to kiss me like you're dying to be inside me, and you can't go on if you don't."

Scoop's nostrils flared, and his eyes dropped to half-mast as his arms slid around her, one cupping her ass, giving it a light squeeze.

"That won't be hard to do. You make me crazy with the things I imagine doing with you. Each taste you've given me during the lessons just makes me crave you more."

His lips claimed hers. His tongue demanding entry as his fingers tunneled into her hair, tilting her head. She didn't think about what was next or what to direct him to do. She gave over to the feelings Scoop ignited. She wasn't sure how long he consumed her, but by the time he stopped, she was a puddle of want. Her breasts ached for his touch.

He pulled away, breathing heavily. "Please do not touch my cock. I don't want to embarrass myself, and one touch from you and I'll come. The taste and feel of you is addictive, and I need a second to calm down."

She smiled, giggled, then snorted. "Mint Chocolate Chip, you couldn't have said anything more perfect. Shall we move to the bed?"

She stepped back, tugging him by the hand toward the bed. She glanced back and saw he'd already turned down the covers and had a couple of condoms on the side table.

He had on pajama bottoms which highlighted that V at his hips she couldn't get enough of. She vowed sometime on this trip she was exploring every inch of it with her tongue. She'd seriously neglected that area when she'd given him a blowjob, but honestly, she'd been so hot to taste him, she'd rushed to the finish. She'd put on a short nightie with cute panties while in the bathroom.

Scoop stepped up closer, backing her legs against the bed. "What next?"

She swallowed, then worked to get the words out. "I think you need to take our clothes off. Part of the fun of being together is unwrapping the present."

"You are a present for me, Sarah. I promise I'll treat you as the gift you are." His words hit her right in the heart. Each day with Scoop had convinced her he was the man for her, but she wasn't sure her being older would work with them. Six years wasn't even considered if the man was older, but when the woman was, sometimes people weren't kind.

His fingers slid under the strap, rasping against her shoulder. She turned her face up to his. Scoop couldn't hide his emotions each time he saw her nude, and she was cherishing every second of their time together.

The strap slid down her arm and his fingers pulled the fabric off her breast.

"You're absolute perfection. Your skin is this creamy color. Then I get to see these beauties." His hand slid under her breast, lifting it. "And these gorgeous rose-colored nipples, all hard for me, just waiting for my tongue to wrap around them."

She lifted her chest. His words inflamed her, but she needed his lips. "Suck them, Rocky Road."

He grinned and nodded. "Your wish is my command, Firecracker."

"Firecracker?"

His lips nibbled across her breast until they reached her nipple. Then his warm mouth engulfed it, sucking hard. He squeezed it lightly while he was sucking, and she could almost come from the feelings he was igniting.

"Yep. A firecracker calmly goes about its day just hanging out until it's ignited. You exude this calm, nurturing personality until someone sets you off. Then boom, you ignite. But it's like a controlled burn to take care of business, burning bright until you accomplish your job."

She vaguely noticed his other hand sliding her other strap off as she listened to his voice rumbling against her skin until the nightie puddled around her feet. She couldn't believe he'd noticed so much about her. He saw her. Not just what she showed everyone else but her core.

His fingers tweaked the nipple he'd uncovered. He slid his lips across her breasts. "Wouldn't want this one to feel neglected," he murmured against her flesh before tugging her nipple into his mouth.

She grasped his shoulders, holding on. "Oh, Scoop," she moaned.

His hands divested her of her panties and him of his pajama pants before sliding his hands under her butt. "Hold on," he directed as he lifted her against him and placing one knee on the bed, so he could lie her down.

"Now, what's next? Do I finally get to taste your pussy, or should I pay more attention to other areas? I'm an overachiever. I need the A. My self-esteem can't handle a failing grade."

Scoop's dirty talk really did it for her. If this wasn't teaching him about sex, she'd have him inside her already. She was wet enough, and he'd made her hot enough it was going to take hardly anything for her to come.

She motioned toward her core. "There's no grade this time. This is all about learning what feels good. Final exam will be later. Yes, you get to taste my pussy. You want to start light and lick all around my clit. Listen to sounds and watch the movements. Each woman is different, and you have to figure out what works best for them."

She hated thinking about him with anyone else, but it was the situation she was in, for now.

He nodded. "Promise me you'll tell me what feels good and what doesn't. Feel free to grab my hair and direct me where you want my mouth. Can I use my fingers?"

"Yes. You can nibble, lick and suck to your heart's content."

She started to open her legs, but Scoop's hands were there, smoothing up her thighs, opening her up. The cooler room air against her core, letting her know he could see everything. No man had ever examined her as closely except her gynecologist. Scoop kissed up her thigh and breathed deep as he got to the seam of her leg. "You smell so good."

His finger traced her, and then he leaned down and followed the path with his tongue. Sarah shivered and started to close her eyes but then forced them open. She didn't want to miss a second of Scoop and what he was doing to her.

His lips and tongue licked, sucked, and feasted on her, building a need she'd never felt before. His fingers were lightly tracing her opening, and the conflicting sensations of the hard suction and the trailing of his fingers had her shooting toward her orgasm. His fingers breaching her opening had her rushing over the top and calling his name as she came. She'd expected him to stop when she came, but he continued kissing and rubbing her which built her need again.

"Oh fuck, Rocky Road, are you sure you haven't done this before?" she groaned.

He chuckled against her, tracing all around her clit before placing a kiss against it. "You're a really good teacher and so fucking sexy when you come but I have always been a fast learner."

She reached down, grasping his shoulder, tugging lightly to have him crawl up her body.

"How about you put on a condom and get inside me? I ache for you."

He reached across her, his hand brushing her breast as he grabbed the condom from the side table. Ripping the package open, he efficiently slid it on his hard, weeping cock. He may not have had sex before, but she'd bet money he'd practiced putting a condom on as proficient as he was.

He leaned closer, one arm holding him up while his other guided his cock to her entrance. He swallowed, closed his eyes, and then muttered, "Please let me last more than one pump."

Sarah giggled, and Scoop's eyes popped open. "Fuck, I said that out loud."

His adorable blush flushed across his cheeks. She reached up to his face, placing her palm against his cheek.

"It's okay. I don't expect you to last. We have plenty of time for you to have control. Now, slide your big cock inside me, Rocky Road, and let's get rid of that pesky virginity."

He nodded and notched his cock at her entrance. She was so ready to have him inside her, and honestly, he might come fast, but she was primed. Everything about him turned her on, and him feasting on her had her aching for more.

His other hand came down beside her shoulder as he pushed in. Heat flared in his eyes and a deeper flush spread across his cheekbones. "Oh, you feel so incredible."

Scoop didn't pull and push in a little. He did one slow glide in until he was fully seated, and she was so full. He leaned closer and his chest hair brushed her turgid nipples, sending another wave of want through her. He glided out and pushed back in.

"Scoop, you won't hurt me, and I need you so bad. Please go harder and faster."

He nodded at her, and then she gave over to the feelings of him thrusting inside her. Seconds later, her eyes closed as everything exploded, and her pussy clamped around Scoop. Never had she felt this way.

If he walked away when this was over, she'd have to figure out how to get along without him. She wasn't sure it was possible.

Chapter Seventeen

Scoop lay quietly with Sarah's head on his shoulder. He hadn't slept a wink last night. After finally making love with Sarah, he'd had too many thoughts running through his head. Being inside her and making her his cemented knowing in his heart and his head that he'd do anything to have her forever.

So many times during the night, he'd wanted to wake her up, but he was worried if he did, he'd blurt out his feelings in a moment of weakness.

Today, they were leaving town for Canton and Fiestaware shopping. After shopping, he was looking forward to making Sarah scream in pleasure and not worry about anyone next door hearing them.

He didn't know if it was because he loved Sarah, but surely, people didn't always feel this way after having sex? How would they get anything done? He wanted to kiss, lick, and explore every inch of her creamy skin. Taking his time to pay homage to each inch as he uncovered it.

He was positive if he looked in the mirror, he'd have the same love-dazed look he'd seen in Bear's and War's eyes after they'd fallen for their women. He couldn't imagine a life without Sarah in it. Heck, he couldn't imagine not waking up beside her tomorrow.

He only had a room at the clubhouse, so they could live in her house. He hadn't been in it before, but knowing Sarah, it was homey with the kitchen as the heart of the home. Cooking and baking for people demonstrated her love language of gifts.

It's one of the reasons he'd known getting her gifts at the author signing would mean so much to her.

Their room smelled of them and sex. His dick hardened as he remembered how Sarah felt clamped around him when she came.

It was more than his first time having sex. It was special because it was Sarah. Each time he touched her skin, he was caressing the woman he wanted forever. He wanted her to meet his mom and his sisters. He could see them all getting along.

If he could imagine the perfect life, he and Sarah would live in her house because he could do his job for the MC anywhere. They'd settle down with an animal or two and a couple of kids. He wanted any kids he had to have siblings. He loved his sisters deeply and couldn't imagine not having them in his life. His mom would fall in love with Bluff Creek and his MC family, so she'd decide to stay in Bluff Creek permanently. Rose and Tasha would decide they wanted to move to Bluff Creek also. Tasha could either work for the MC or work at the hospital in Coldwater. Rose could join the sheriff's office. He knew the sheriff and was positive Rose would be welcomed with open arms and not looked down on for being a woman or she could go to work with Sarah's sisters. The possibilities were endless. Now he had to figure out how to get everyone on board with his idea.

For now, he'd cherish the feel and scent of Sarah in his arms and cuddled up on his shoulder. He was grateful she hadn't held the puking against him. He'd never been so happy in his life.

He glanced at the clock. Not long until they needed to get up and shower. He was hoping Sarah would be willing to shower together after he'd been inside her, but he would let her lead. He was going to win her heart, mind, and soul. He just had to figure out what his woman needed to believe they could have forever.

SARAH IGNORED THE TEXTS as long as she could. Her sisters had texted about the book signing, but then had started pestering her if she and Scoop had as they so eloquently put it: shagged, banged, boinked, had a hot beef injection, bumped uglies, cleaned cobwebs from the womb room or rode the beef bus.

She loved her sisters and today, she had to keep reminding herself of that. She shared a lot with them, but last night was more than she expected.

Thank goodness they had plans to visit an automobile museum and some antique malls today. Hopefully, they'd stay busy because she was seriously overthinking everything about Scoop.

Last night had been perfect. No, more than perfect. When he'd been inside her, every dream she ever had was fulfilled. Scoop inside her had been more than having sex, though she wouldn't go as far as calling it making love. It had been something more than a lesson.

She wasn't sure how she was supposed to be just friends afterwards. He hadn't dated anyone since he came to the MC, but what if he started when they went back? How could her heart survive seeing him with someone else? His lips on someone else's or his arms around someone else.

They'd been on the road nine days and her whole life was forever changed. When she'd woken up on Scoop's shoulder this morning, she'd known she was in over her head. She'd been dreaming of a little boy with his eyes and brown curls and a little girl with her blonde hair.

She hadn't fallen for Scoop instantly, but this love part had snuck up on her. One second, she'd been positive she'd keep her heart intact, and then, it hit her with the force of an EF5 tornado. A total annihilation of her defenses. One second, her walls had been strong, and the next, she'd been wondering how she'd survive going back to just being friends.

Her best bet to survive was acting as if nothing had changed. They had five days left. She'd be completely fine. She'd give him his final tonight and then they could go back to being friends the rest of the trip.

Despite how wonderful he was, he was six years younger, and he might not want her for forever, only for now. She wanted him, but unless he gave her an indication this was more than sex, she'd have to stick to their friends only plan.

Final tonight. Then they could spend the rest of the trip just hanging out as friends to prepare her for when she got back.

Chapter Eighteen

Sarah eased the door to their room closed. Scoop was still asleep, and she had to get away. Last night had changed everything. Having him do a final to show off his skills had seemed a cute, harmless way for them to end their trip and to give her some space from her feelings.

When she'd originally added it to her list before they left town, she'd wanted to give him confidence after spending the trip teaching him. Every time she thought of last night, her heart pounded, and she had trouble breathing. She'd been positive she could go back to being friends if needed, but she'd seriously underestimated how much he meant to her.

Every touch and taste had chipped away at her last piece of resistance. It hadn't been a final. It had been Rocky Road showing how he felt about her with each caress.

She'd promised herself that no matter how much she liked him that at the end of their time, she'd go back to being friends. He was one of her best friends and co-workers, but last night had cemented what she now knew. She'd been lying to herself. It had become so much more and there was no way she could go back. How had she screwed up her life this much?

When she pictured what she wanted, he was in every scene, but how could she change their friendship?

She walked toward the hotel's breakfast area and called Winnie. Maybe she could help. The phone rang then went to voicemail. Glancing at the time, she realized Winnie was probably busy with the kids. She tried Jesse next.

"Hey Sarah, how's the trip?" Jesse's voice had her fighting tears. Her sisters would help her.

"I don't know what to do." Sarah didn't fight the quiver in her voice. How was she going to do this?

"Okay, we've got this. Give me a second." Sarah waited while Jesse did something. Sarah watched the people getting breakfast, wondering if she could stomach anything.

"Sarah, I added Winnie, Beth, and Remi. What do you need?"

What did she need? She needed to freaking go back two weeks and not agree to this stupid plan. Then everything would be fine.

"Sarah, whatever it is, we'll try to help." Beth's voice washed over her. Her sisters had her back and could look at her situation objectively.

"Last night, I had Rocky Road have a final, but it didn't feel like a final."

"What did it feel like?" Remi coaxed.

"It felt like everything I've always wanted, but it's not what we agreed to. What if he doesn't want more?"

"But what if he's feeling exactly as you are this morning? I've always thought he felt more for you. The way he watches you when you walk into a room and his eyes follow you." With Beth's surveillance skills, she would notice stuff like that.

"Really?"

"Sarah, I love that you're so nurturing to everyone, but sometimes, you spend so much time taking care of others that you miss what is in front of you. Maybe it's time you grabbed a spoon and dug into all that Scoop has to offer." Jesse was the last sister she'd expected to tell her to take a chance. Jesse had always said she wasn't sure if she wanted a family and kids.

Sarah had always known she wanted a family. If she could oversee tech and have a big family, she'd be thrilled. She wanted to be at home when the kids came home from school and be available for every parent volunteer opportunity. She wanted her kids to have what her mom had given to her. Could she take the chance with Mint Chocolate Chip?

"What about our age difference?"

Winnie's laughter came through the line.

"It's not like you're ninety and he's thirty. It's six years. Besides, Scoop's not your average guy. He had to grow up early. He's as mature as any of the older guys."

Maybe Winnie was right. With Scoop's home life, he'd been forced to mature earlier.

"So what do I do? I want it all." Sarah waited for her sisters. She trusted they'd make sense of what she was going through.

"It's like Jesse said. You have to take a chance and make the move. Go back in that room and grab on. Show him what you want and then talk about it in the car. I mean, you're on a road trip. It's not like he can get away from you." Beth's words calmed the last fears she had.

If she wanted more with Rocky Road, then she had to let him know. She couldn't expect him to read her mind. She walked back toward the room as her sisters moved to other topics.

Winnie was threatening to ban Beth from her house if she brought the kids and dogs any more toys.

"Okay, guys, I'm at the room. I'm going to do what you said. I can do this. If I don't, I'll always regret it. Thanks for always having my back. Love you."

Echoes of 'love you too' sounded as they each ended the call. Sarah slid her key in and quietly opened the door. The loud music coming from the bathroom had her peeking around the opened door.

They listened to a lot of ABBA on the trip because Scoop's mom had loved it when he was growing up and he'd fallen in love with the music. She wasn't sure his mom should know what Scoop was doing while listening to the song.

He was fresh from the shower with droplets still sliding down his chest. He had a towel around his neck, and he was moving his hips to the beat of the song. His one arm was up in the air as he danced around the room. His cock was hitting each thigh as he danced.

The feast for her eyes had her biting her lip. Even goofing around, she found him enticing. When he turned around and shook his butt toward the mirror, she couldn't help but admire those muscles of his she'd touched and tasted.

He turned back toward the mirror and opened his eyes as he danced. His eyes widened as they caught her reflection in the mirror. His cheeks pinkened then she saw when he decided to say fuck it. He dropped the towel from his neck and stepped out and grabbed her hand. He spun her around then pulled her close.

For once in her life, she didn't think about anything but the fun of being with Rocky Road and letting him guide her around the room. The first song ended, and he continued dancing with her as another ABBA song started. This one was a little slower. He pulled her close, kissing her ear. She didn't care she was fully dressed, and he was nude. All she cared about is that he had her in his arms.

"So, I have to ask. What prompted your dance in the bathroom?"

Scoop's blush deepened and spread to his chest. He spun her away and then brought her back close to him. For not having any experience dancing when they started their trip, he'd definitely picked up some moves.

"I was celebrating. Giving him kudos for not coming as soon as I got inside you last night. As luscious and amazing as you are, that's a big deal."

Sarah bit her lip, trying not to giggle, but honestly, his words were hilarious. "So, it was a penis party or a cock celebration?"

Scoop pulled her closer, brushing his lips across hers. "You think you're funny, don't you?"

"Maybe."

"You can call it whatever you want as long as I don't have to give up being with you."

Sarah stared at Scoop trying to figure out what exactly he was saying. Did he want more sex? Or was there more behind his words?

"I'm going to get dressed, then we can grab some breakfast before we get on the road. We want to make sure we get to the cabin before it's dark. I read the directions, but it looked like cell coverage might be spotty there, and I'd rather not have to find it in the dark."

Scoop slid his underwear up, then slid his jeans on. He had his shoes and shirt on and had grabbed his keys and wallet.

"Sarah, you ready for breakfast?"

She nodded at Scoop. She'd focus on breakfast and then figure out how to talk to Scoop about their relationship.

Chapter Nineteen

Sarah looked around the cabin they had rented. It was gorgeous. A couple of ponds to fish in and close enough to town they could head in to eat if they wanted. She'd spent a chunk of cash on the Fiestaware she'd found, but she didn't care. She'd found one of the retired dancing lady cookie jars. Her mom had one, but Remi got it when they divided everything. Sarah had also found an entertaining set which Scoop's eyes had widened at when she'd paid for it. He'd been amazed how much what he called a relish tray would cost. He'd won the best boyfriend award when he said as long as she liked it, who cared how much it cost.

Not that he was really her boyfriend, but for the trip, he was. She couldn't wait until they got everything unloaded because after she showered, she was jumping him. She'd loved shopping, but seeing his ass in his jeans all day made her want to lick every inch of him, including that big, gorgeous cock of his. She'd left it alone because he'd been worried he'd come too soon last time, but she was getting another taste. Him coming would be the goal, and he could get hard again.

Scoop's phone ringing from the counter had her checking who was calling. Tasha calling. She yelled Scoop's name, but he didn't answer. He said he was going to double check the generator the property had. He'd mentioned he was going to check in with his sisters because he hadn't heard from them. She'd answer because what if they needed something.

"Hello?"

"Is Derek there?" Tasha's voice quivered, and she sounded like she was crying.

"Yes, this is Sarah. He's outside, but let me get him. Are you okay?"

"Hurry. No, I'm not and neither's Rose. We need help."

Sarah ran outside, pulling the phone away from her mouth. "Scoop!" she yelled.

Scoop ran out from behind the shed where the generator was. "What?"

She pressed the speaker button on the phone. "Tasha, Scoop's here."

"Derek. Rose is missing. The police won't do anything. I think they might be in on it. She had a shift early this morning. I dropped her off because her car wouldn't start. I saw her walk into the station. When I went to pick her up, her partner was there but said she never showed. I don't trust him and neither does Rose. You have to help. I freaking told her to tell you what was going on." Her words trailed off as she sobbed.

Scoop took a deep breath. "Tasha. We'll find her. Where are you?"

"I'm in my car, sitting outside the police station."

While Scoop was getting information about Tasha, Sarah pulled her phone out and called Gage, War and Roam's younger brother, who was a member of the Texas Chapter of the Bluff Creek Brotherhood MC. She knew him best. They'd been in high school together.

He answered on the first ring, and she stepped away and informed him of what was going on. The sisters lived in Dallas and the Texas Chapter was located in a small town a couple of hours away. Gage ran their brewery and was luckily meeting with a couple of bars in Dallas on a sales call. Sarah walked closer, listening to Tasha cry for her sister was heartbreaking but not what was needed. Sarah leaned closer, knowing what she was going to do might anger Scoop, but it was needed.

"Hey, Tasha, this is Sarah. I work with Scoop and also help run my family's security company."

Scoop glared at Sarah.

"I need you to pull it together. Once we have Rose back, we can fall apart. Gage, who is one of the brothers with the Texas Chapter of Scoop's MC, is in Dallas and about twenty minutes away. I want you to keep your doors locked, follow all the traffic laws because we don't want you stopped, and head to the large convenience store on Highway 66. Do you know where he's talking about?"

Tasha sniffed, then answered, "Yes."

"Once you get there, check around and then get inside the store as quickly as possible. Tell the clerk you need to wait by them because you had a strange car following you. Say your boyfriend is on the way and you don't need the police. Gage isn't in his cut because he was doing sales calls. I'm going to send you a picture of him. Now, tell me what you're going to do."

"I'm going to head to the big convenience store on Highway 66, not stopping for anything but not speeding. I'm going to check my surroundings, then go in and tell the clerk a strange car is following me but my boyfriend is coming so I don't need the police."

"You got it. Now, Gage will keep you safe and Scoop and I will come to you. Once you get to Gage, he's going to quiz you about all the things that have been strange for Rose, and then we'll get her back."

"Okay," she sniffed again, then hung up.

Scoop turned toward her, fire in his eyes. She held her hand up, dialing Gage.

"She's on her way. I'm sending her a picture of you. She's scared, but I think she'll hold it together until you get there. Do you have a safe place?"

"Yep, we'll be heading to one of our properties. Bootstrap is coordinating and Cowboy is searching traffic cams around the precinct to give us leads. Salty, Dodge, and Blue are heading toward town and will meet us at the building. They want you to call if you can think of anything to help. I called Dad and he's mobilizing Bluff Creek to back us up if needed. I'll text when I have Tasha, then get info from her. Scoop, brother, we'll get her back."

"Thanks, Gage. Tasha and Rose are both tough, but I can't lose either of them."

Sarah slid her arm around Scoop even though she could tell he was irritated with her telling Tasha she had to get it together.

"Now, let's get loaded back up. You can yell and get after me in the truck."

Sarah pulled Scoop behind her up the stairs and into the cabin to grab their stuff. Who knows how soon after Tasha dropped her off that Rose went missing. Time was against them and they needed to get on the road.

She grabbed the items she'd unpacked and stuffed them back in the bag. Thank goodness they hadn't unpacked much yet. She wanted to get on the road so one of them could start searching for a thread to follow.

They had the truck packed and the cabin locked. She texted the owners to let them know something had come up and they wouldn't be staying. She paused by the door.

"Scoop, I need to know where your head is at. Where will you do best? Driving or researching? I'm good with either."

Scoop sent her another glare, pulled the keys out of his pocket, and walked around toward the driver's side. Okay, she'd research. She grabbed her computer, laptop desk, and a couple suckers from the bag, then flipped her phone to a hotspot.

She got settled and put her seatbelt on. Scoop backed out of the parking space by the cabin, then floored the gas. The Bronco slid and fishtailed on the gravel road. If he thought him being an ass driving would worry her, then he really didn't know her as well as he thought. She'd been around her sisters when they were all on their period and pissy as all get out.

He was upset and feeling helpless. She'd do some digging, and they'd wait for Gage to let them know he had Tasha. She'd give him time to think through options, and she was positive he would click into problem-solving mode in a little bit. If not, she'd knock some sense into him.

Chapter Twenty

Scoop focused on driving the last couple of miles to their destination. They were meeting Gage, Tasha, and the brothers from the Texas Chapter at a property they owned outside of Dallas.

Cowboy had picked up Rose being put in a van six hours into her shift when the police car she and her partner were in stopped at a storage unit. The partner was in on it because he walked away after Rose was taken and went back to work. The van had been picked up on traffic cams taking Rose to a bar near where they were meeting. Cowboy was researching who owned it. It hadn't been on their radar before, so they didn't have intel on it. Rose was carried in the front door which told them no one had cared about an unconscious woman being brought in.

He'd gotten over being mad at Sarah. He'd realized she had done what needed to be done, getting Tasha focused on keeping herself safe. He'd been an ass, but he'd helped take care of his sisters from when they were little. Sometimes they felt more like his kids than his sisters.

The overwhelming fear for what Rose could be going through ran like a movie in his head. He pulled up to the gate at the property and entered the code Gage had given them. He pulled over to where Gage's brewery van was parked. Sarah started to get out, and he grabbed her hand to stop her.

"I'm sorry, I was an ass. I was..."

Sarah held up her hand, bringing it to his cheek. "It's okay. You're scared. Now, let's get in there and get a plan together to get your sister back."

Sarah opened the door and had her bag over her shoulder with an inquiring look. He grabbed his backpack with his computer and weapon and followed her inside.

The building looked dilapidated, with peeling paint on the outside, but the inside was clean, with sealed cement for the floor. A couple tables were to the side with plans laid out on them. Gage was with a couple of the Texas Chapter members, looking at monitors set up on a table. Tasha was standing near them. He hurried over to her, pulling her into his chest.

"Derek, they've had her for six hours," she cried out and shook against his chest.

"I know, but we know where she is, so we'll get her out. I love you, but I need to find out what we're doing."

She nodded, "Okay."

He walked over to the screens, where Sarah was looking through the footage. He walked up as she asked, "Did you get the stuff?"

Gage rolled his eyes and motioned to one of the guys with Prospect on his vest. He walked over and handed her the bags.

"Baby girl, we haven't decided if that's the best plan yet."

"Bootstrap, you know it's the best chance we have of getting information on where she's being held. We can go on one of the guys' bikes. We stage a fight in the parking lot, and he yells at me and tells me to find my own way home. I go in to get something while I wait for my ride. I'll ask to use the bathroom and check the place out."

"What? No, I don't want you in danger." Scoop didn't like raising his voice, but he'd already lost his sister. He wasn't losing Sarah too.

"You all act like this is the first time I've gone undercover. Beth may be our disguise guru, but we've all played a part multiple times. Besides, if you got what I asked, all they're going to notice is boobs. Trust me. I bet they won't even look at my face. I'm going to get dressed. You'll be able to see and hear everything. When I'm ready to get out, whoever is playing my boyfriend can come back and do this big apology in the main room while you all rescue her. It's a sound plan. Now, I'm changing. Get with the fucking program and fine tune any issues while I'm gone."

Scoop watched her stride over, grab a bag, and go into the bathroom. Tasha slid close to him, and he wrapped his arm around her. They had to get Rose back.

"You guys know she's our best chance. They'll see a short blonde with big boobs, and trust me, I've seen her playing the part. They won't have any idea what she's doing, and she's right. They won't be even looking at her face. Their eyes will be on her boobs and ass." Gage stared at him, waiting for Scoop to get on board with the plan.

"She's not going in there without weapons. She had us bring her a Beretta 3032 Tomcat for her boot and a knife for the other boot. I also included one of our self-defense whip bracelets I've been making in my spare time," Dodge punctuated his words with a shoulder pat. "She won't be defenseless."

Tasha's arm squeezed a little tighter around him, her hand patting his chest. He had to remind himself that Sarah had trained as much as her sisters, but this time was the first time someone he loved was going into harm's way. But it was the only way they could get eyes inside. He couldn't let Rose stay there any longer. He'd held them as babies and sang to them to get them to sleep.

He'd helped change their diapers. He'd taught them how to drive, how to use a gun, and how to watch out for boys wanting only one thing. Even though he was only ten years older than them, once their dad left, he'd been a mini dad to them.

Each hour increased the chance Rose was being abused or hurt. He needed her out of there.

Sarah walked, no, strutted back in. He was petrified for Rose, but his woman looked hot. Tight black leather riding pants cupped every curve of her butt and thighs. Motorcycle boots with silver buckles were on her feet. A steel plate across the front would offer a little more protection if she ended up having to fight her way out of there. She'd braided her hair so there was nothing obscuring the view of her breasts. The tight tank top was so thin, he could see the outline of her nipples through it. He could see the bra strap, but he couldn't figure out how her nipples were showing through.

There was very little they all couldn't see about her breasts. He didn't like it, but he agreed with Sarah. They'd only be looking at one thing. She walked over to the table, pointedly ignoring him. He'd been a little loud about her going in, but he didn't want her hurt. She could take care of herself, but he didn't have to like her going into danger.

She efficiently slid the gun in her right boot and the knife in her left. Dodge was showing her how the whip bracelet wrapped around her arm and how to quickly unfurl it to use it. She wrapped it around her left arm.

"So, who's taking me there?" Sarah popped her hip out with her hand on it. Her attitude screamed badass, a side he'd only seen once when they'd helped Remi and War during an incident.

Bootstrap pointed at Dodge. "Dodge will be the one playing your boyfriend. Cowboy is monitoring. He's got the necklace you'll be wearing so we can monitor. We'll stage in two areas. The prospect will stay here with Tasha. Scoop, if you're positive you can keep calm, I think you'd best serve us on the takedown crew. Rose will recognize you. I don't want any delays getting her out of there because she doesn't trust us."

"I'm solid."

SARAH RELAXED AT SCOOP'S words. She hadn't wanted to spend time fighting about whether or not she should go in. They needed to have first-hand knowledge of what condition Rose was in. Six hours was a long time and every minute counted.

Sarah slid the short motorcycle jacket on over her tank top. They'd still be able to see an impressive amount of her boobage. She'd always been annoyed how she received a more than generous amount compared to her sisters, but today, if it helped her get Rose back, she'd be thankful. She picked up the half helmet and followed Dodge out to his motorcycle. He'd taken off his cut and replaced it with a plain black leather jacket. He'd switched into a long sleeve shirt to cover up the Bluff Creek Brotherhood MC tattoo on his arm.

She took a deep breath and walked over to Scoop who followed them outside along with the rest of the members who were going. She leaned up breathing deep his scent. It always calmed her, and she could use any help she could get today.

She brushed her lips against his. "We'll get her back."

As she started to walk away, her hand was grasped and tugged back. Scoop's arms wrapped around her, his body shaking as he held her.

"Firecracker, you keep yourself safe. I can't imagine life without you and don't plan on having to. Love you!"

At Scoop's words, she jerked her eyes to his. So many emotions blazing in them, but they didn't have time for this right now. He set her helmet on her head and buckled it. He kissed her on her nose, turned her toward Dodge on his bike and tapped her ass to send her on her way.

"Let's get this done."

Sarah held tight to Dodge even though she'd rather be behind Scoop. This was a mission. She'd been on plenty with her sisters, and each time, her stomach churned. Today, it was roiling because this was Scoop's little sister. Sure, at twenty-five, Rose wasn't a child. As an older sibling herself, Sarah could imagine what Scoop was going through. He was feeling powerless, scared out of his mind at what could be happening to her and regret at not pushing Rose to share more about the situation.

If, no, *when* they got Rose out of there, Sarah was positive Rose would be hearing a lecture from Scoop about leaning on your family. Dodge tapped her thigh, indicating he was turning in to the bar's parking lot. Show time. She'd channel all her anger and worry about Rose into the best fight ever.

Dodge pulled into the middle of the parking lot, stopping the motorcycle but not getting off. Sarah hopped off, anger in every step. Turning to Dodge she ripped the helmet off her head.

"You ass!" she screeched. "You pledge you'll love me forever, then sleep with that skank."

Dodge got off the motorcycle, holding his hands up. "Now, babe, it was only a couple of times. It didn't mean nothing."

She stomped her foot, screaming in apparent frustration. She needed at least one person to see their act. "A couple. Are you fucking kidding me? I thought it was only once. I don't need your shit."

"Babe, c'mon. Calm down." Dodge walked toward her.

At the sound of the door of the bar opening, Sarah started backing up. "You stay away from me. I'm not doing this again. I'll find my own fucking way home."

"Hey, what's going on out here?"

Sarah turned to see who was talking. It wasn't one of the guys who had abducted Rose, but he was in the bar where she was being held. As far as Sarah was concerned, he was the enemy. He was tall with a barrel chest. He had on motorcycle boots, ripped dirty jeans and an unbuttoned mechanic's shirt over a white undershirt. He had his hair tied back with a bandana and if he'd washed it in the last week, Sarah would be surprised.

"Who I thought was my man decided this," Sarah ran her hands across the side of her boobs down her waist and over her butt, "wasn't enough to keep him happy. He'd rather have a wandering dick."

"Now, babe..."

"If you call me babe one more time..."

Before Sarah could finish, her rescuer decided to intervene.

"Man, you're not welcome here. She doesn't want you around, and I definitely don't want you here. Get gone."

Dodge put on a good act, huffing around as he got back on his bike. Right before he fired it up, he made one more effort. "Just give me another chance, babe."

Sarah stomped her feet, pointing him toward the street adding an exasperated scream for good measure. She hoped her rescuer was buying her act. Dodge started to pull out, flipping her a one-finger salute to seal his act.

"Don't want to call you babe because dickhead did. What should I call you, sugar? You want to come in?"

She stared into his eyes a bit. She didn't want to seem too easy. She nodded, "Yes. I really need the bathroom. I'd been asking him to stop for the last twenty minutes. Then that bitch's text came through on his phone. When I saw that, I just saw fucking red. And it's Beretta but Retta for short."

He held the door open as she walked in and immediately scanned and catalogued the area for threats and exits. A group of men sitting at a booth. Two men playing pool. A bartender wiping down the bar. A flashing sign indicated the restroom.

"Retta, I'm going to need the story about your name and the ladies' room is back that way."

"Oh, it's a good one. I'll be happy to share as soon as I'm a little more comfortable. Gonna also splash some water on my face and see if I can cool my temper a little since I still want to smack someone upside the head."

On the outside, Sarah made sure she looked the part, but on the inside, she was planning what she'd do if things went wrong. She stepped into the hallway. The men's restroom was first, then another unmarked door followed by the women's restroom. The other side of the hall had a room marked office and one marked storage. She hoped Rose wasn't there. If she was, Sarah would have a hard time communicating with her. The bartender had a perfect view of the hallway.

Sarah took note that the back door to the bar directly beside women's restroom didn't have an alarm when it was opened. There was a key lock and a deadbolt but not much else. She pushed open the door, walking in slowly. She checked both stalls and then looked in the mirror, pretending to talk to herself as she studied the room for surveillance. She had to chance it. She slid her hand down into her jacket, pulling out the device to check for recording devices just far enough to see the display and use it. It came back negative. There was a small vent that was high on the wall. As the shortest sister, she didn't have the option of whispering directly into the vent.

"Rose, I'm with your brother and we know you've been taken. Are you in there?"

The sound of metal scraping across a cement floor drifted through the vent.

"Yes."

"Are you hurt?" Sarah hoped Rose had just been knocked out to get her here and that they'd left her alone otherwise.

"Just a little bumped and bruised. I can still fight if needed."

Sarah wished she were taller like Remi. If so, she could have reached the vent to unscrew it and given Rose her knife.

"Okay, we're working on a plan to get you out. Hold on. I'm going to see if I can get any more info, then we'll be coming. Be ready and stay strong."

Sarah splashed some more water on her face, then dried her hands. "Okay, guys, I'm heading out into the room. Give me a couple minutes to assess the firepower they have, then send Dodge back."

She wished she knew if they were receiving her. She was missing the ear pieces she wore on jobs. With the rush to get Rose, whoever had been in charge of the equipment hadn't grabbed any.

She took a deep breath and walked back out into the main room. The guy who'd come outside was over near one of the booths, leaning against it talking with two men sitting at a table nearby. Sarah saw how the men were listening to his every word. She'd bet money he was the big dog in charge of everything.

"Thanks for letting me freshen up." Sarah held out her hand. "Beretta James but Retta to my friends."

His rough hand grasped hers. "Folks around here call me Stroke."

She smiled, nodding, "Bet that one's got a good story too."

He motioned to the booth. She didn't want to sit in the booth because it made her vulnerable but couldn't figure out an excuse why. So she sat but didn't slide in. She didn't want anyone beside her. She turned so she could include the men at the table in her story.

"Sugar, we're waiting."

Sarah nodded. "Daddy wanted all of us girls to know how to shoot a gun. He had a mechanic shop at the edge of town where he worked late. Momma was gone long before I was old enough to even remember her. He took me out back of the house when I was ten. That was when my sisters learned. He had all these pistols to try with. Y'all know that saying can't hit the broad side of a barn?" She waited while they nodded. "That was me with every pistol he had. I don't know whether it was the kickback or the way the grip was, but I was horrible. Which really sucked because my sisters were all crack shots. I'm the youngest. Gah, I got so tired of being called the baby."

Sarah rolled her eyes for effect. A guy from the pool table had come over to listen. All the better for her team to get Rose out.

"By now, I am crying because Daddy is getting frustrated. I mean, the man had to be a saint to raise five girls after my momma left, but he was about done. He looked me in the eye and said, 'Louise, girl, I need you to try a little harder. You have to be able to protect yourself.' By this time, I'm worried. I hated being the baby and now, if I couldn't figure out how to shoot a gun, my sissies would never let me hear the end of it. I could imagine their voices echoing Baby Louise until the end of time. I mean, don't get me wrong. I love my sissies, but that doesn't mean they don't stomp on my last nerve sometimes. So he hands me one last gun, a 92SF Compact L Beretta. Now this gun I could actually hold in my hand without it hurting my wrist. I held the gun up. Daddy turned me and had me change my stance. Then he told me to take a deep breath in, breathe out slow and squeeze the trigger slowly. I followed his direction and hit the target dead center. Boom! Not the edge but dead center. Daddy took the gun out of my hand and laid it on the stump. He grabbed me and swung me around. I was just so happy he was pleased with me."

The men were nodding along with her story. Her watch vibrated, letting her know Dodge would be coming in.

"He looked at me and said, 'I never liked the name Louise. Your skank of a mother chose it, but girly, you are all me. You're my little Beretta.' My sisters shortened it to Retta because one of the tight-ass teachers wouldn't call me by it at school. She said it was inappro-priate." Sarah drawled the word out and rolled her eyes, shaking her breasts a little to have all eyes on her.

"That's a fuckin' great name. Screw that teacher," one of the men commented.

The bang of a door heralded Dodge walking back in. "Babe, I can't leave it like this."

Stroke stood up and walked toward Dodge, with the other men following him. She scooted out of the booth and followed behind. Her watch vibrated with a text.

Working on door.

"I don't think she wants to listen to you," Stroke stated with his arms crossed.

"Yeah, pussy, we kinda like her. She can stay."

Dodge put his hand on his heart. "Babe, I fucked up. You are the best thing that has ever happened to me, and I didn't treasure you like I should. If you give me a chance, I promise I will take care of your heart."

If the situation wasn't so dire, Sarah might really appreciate how suave Dodge was with the women. She stood and put her hand on her hip. She hadn't gotten the all-clear yet, so she needed to drag this out.

"How do I know you won't trip again and let your dick fall into some other woman? I deserve a man who puts me first."

A couple of the guys laughed. The bartender was invested in their drama and hadn't once glanced toward the hallway.

"I deserve that. But if you don't give me another chance, you might miss out on the best thing to ever happen to you. Babe, we're fire. We'll burn hot at times then settle down to an ember, but no matter what, the fire will always be there."

A small pop sounded from the hallway at the same time the *opening door to Rose* text came through.

She walked around Stroke slowly, then stopped in front of Dodge. She wanted to get out of here but wanted Rose out in the parking lot when she and Dodge left.

"You hurt me, but you're right. I can't just walk away not knowing if you're my one."

Dodge's hand grasped hers and tugged her close to him. "Thank you, babe."

He gave her a squeeze, then turned to the guys. "Sorry I fucked up your day guys, but I need to get my girl home so I can start making up for my asinine ways."

A couple of the guys turned toward the hallway at the sound of another pop, and the bartender glanced toward the hallway. He turned toward the guys and yelled, "Breach!"

Sarah pulled her gun out with her right hand after she had unhooked her bracelet whip to allow it to unfurl. If she and Dodge could get out of here without any bloodshed, she'd be happy. A couple of the guys started running for the hallway.

Sarah had a clear shot, so she shot the floor right in front of the guys.

"No need to check that out. Just a couple of our friends."

"Bitch, thought you seemed off but also figured we could listen to you then use you later."

"Thanks for the offer, but I usually like my guys a little cleaner."

Dodge had his gun out and was keeping an eye on the guys too. They were outnumbered and Sarah knew it was only a matter of time until she and Dodge lost the upper hand. They just needed long enough for Scoop to get Rose out safely.

One of the guys closest to her stepped as if he was going to try to grab her gun. She flicked her wrist like Dodge had made her practice and aimed toward his face. Dodge had cautioned not to send it toward a lower arm or hand because someone could possibly grab the whip and yank her toward them.

The end scraped across the guy's cheek, leaving a trail of blood.

"Bitch!"

"I don't want to hurt you, but I will, if needed. We just want to leave."

Dodge tugged her back toward the door and the men continued advancing, but with both guns on them and the threat of her whip hitting them, they seemed to be biding their time. Dodge opened the door and pushed Sarah out. She saw him grab a couple things from his jacket, then throw them in the room. She saw a couple flashes as the door closed.

Her watched vibrated with *Safe*. She slipped her helmet on and got on behind Dodge. He started the motorcycle and had them out of the parking lot and on the street in seconds. She hoped what she assumed were flash bangs bought them enough time to be hidden before the men could give chase.

He headed toward their safe building at a high enough speed to get away but not attract attention. As he turned the corner to their facility, he made a quick turn into an alley, gliding the motorcycle into a garage where the door closed behind them.

One of the prospects for the Texas Chapter ran outside the garage and moved a red truck and a beat-up car in front of the garage door.

She followed Dodge out of the small door at the front of the garage. She realized they were on the back side of the building and had to walk through what looked like a motorcycle and truck parts yard. It hadn't taken them long, but it seemed like forever since they'd left the bar. She wanted to lay eyes on Scoop and know he and his sister were okay.

She also wanted to be held in his arms. She'd stayed strong, but so much could have gone wrong at the bar and she'd been worried about Scoop.

Chapter Twenty-One

Scoop hadn't ever gone into a situation where two people he loved were in danger. It had taken everything in him to focus on getting Rose out and trust that his brothers had Sarah's back.

Once they'd gotten the door open to the room where Rose was being held, the bartender had yelled breach. He'd gotten his sister out while Bootstrap had kept a gun on the bartender and anyone who considered coming down the hallway. He'd had Rose on the back of his borrowed bike, and they'd been out of the lot with Gage following behind in a car to keep anyone from following.

Rose had been a little shaky when he'd pulled the bike into the complex, so he picked her up and carried her in. By the time they'd rescued her, Butcher, the medic for the Texas Chapter, had arrived.

He'd brought his bag, but they'd already started setting up a medical room in the building. At Butcher's yell, he carried Rose directly in and sat her on the exam table.

He didn't know Butcher, but he was impressed with how he had handled Rose. He told her what he needed to do each time he needed to touch her and asked her if she was okay with it. By the third time, she looked him in the eye and told him just to get it done. She appreciated his touchy-feely way of asking, but she wanted it done.

He started to leave to give them privacy, but Rose asked him to stay. When she'd said they'd drugged her but hadn't taken advantage of her, he breathed a sigh of relief.

Scoop hadn't needed to get after Rose for not calling for help because she was already beating herself up for not telling him what she suspected.

She'd noticed when she and her partner were on patrol there was a weird vibe with the people they talked with in the neighborhoods. A couple times he'd had her drop him somewhere and pick him up when their lunchtime was over. When she'd picked him up, he'd smelled of sex and something else she couldn't identify.

She'd started suspecting her partner and possibly others were involved in slavery. She knew some of the lawmakers tried to call it human trafficking, but Rose had been adamant it was slavery and Scoop agreed. They could try to call it something else to make it not sound as bad, but in reality, enslaving someone whether it be for sexual favors or something else was slavery.

She'd discussed how worried she was with Tasha. Tasha had urged her to call Scoop, but she didn't want to involve him until she had more info. He'd made sure she understood that information was his job.

Butcher finished the last of his tests. "I think drinking lots of fluids and resting will allow the rest of whatever drug they gave you to leave your system. You were gone eight hours, and it sounds like you woke up on your own about seven hours after being administered the drug. If you experience any trouble breathing, a headache or nausea, let me know."

Scoop helped Rose down off the exam table and pulled her into his arms. Butcher opened the door.

"I'll send Tasha in so she can see you're okay."

Scoop didn't say anything. He just held Rose in his arms and opened his arm to allow Tasha in when she joined them. He'd held them as babies, fed them and changed their diapers. Now they were adults, it was hard to know he couldn't keep them both safe indefinitely. He could try and he would be trying. He needed them in Bluff Creek where he could keep an eye on them.

"Rose, I'm glad you're okay, but I'm going to kick your butt when I get over being so scared," Tasha whispered against Rose's cheek. "I fucking can't lose you, Thorny."

"Can't lose you either, Tasha-Basha. I'm not going back there."

Scoop was thrilled to hear he wasn't going to have to fight to get Rose to not go back to the police station. Hearing them call each other their pet names brought back so many memories of their fights. Although the names were said with love now, they used them as weapons when they were younger.

"Let's go out here and see if Sarah's back."

He kept his arms around Rose and Tasha as they walked out to all the men who had his back and helped get his sister back. The MC was the family he'd always wanted. He'd thought he'd find some of the comradery at the police department, but it hadn't been the way he envisioned. With the Bluff Creek Brotherhood, he could truly make a difference.

"Thank you so much."

Bootstrap stood near where Cowboy was monitoring the area.

"We're glad you're okay, baby girl."

Scoop felt Rose's muscles tense. "Chill, Bootstrap calls all women baby girl. It's just him. Don't take offense."

"I'm glad I'm back, too. Thank you all for rescuing me."

"Scoop!" His heart pounded at Sarah's voice. Rose and Tasha slipped out of his arms, and he held them open for his Firecracker.

She smelled of wind and something from the bar, but he didn't care. They were all safe, and for a moment, he was going to relish holding his woman in his arms.

"Thank you."

Sarah leaned back and smiled. "I'm not going to say it was fun because I was worried about Rose, but man, that bracelet whip was awesome."

Rose and Tasha crowded around, "What bracelet whip?"

Sarah smiled, "Glad you're okay, Rose. This."

Sarah pulled back from him and started showing his sisters her bracelet and what it could do.

He turned at Dodge's hand on his shoulder. "She used that whip against the guy who was coming a little close to both of us. It scared them enough to give us the upper hand."

"I have the video if you want to see. She hit him within an inch of his eye," Cowboy yelled.

Scoop shook his head. When he'd come to Bluff Creek with War, he'd never imagined he'd find a woman who could not only keep up with him on hacking and protecting their family but was also a badass who faced down danger at a moment's notice.

And later she'd immerse herself in baking and nurturing her family. He'd had a dream when he first left on the trip. Playing her fake boyfriend to see if what he felt for her was real and having her teach him all the things he'd missed.

When he'd told her he loved her before she went with Dodge, he'd meant it. Somewhere along the way, she'd crawled inside his heart, and he couldn't imagine a life without her in it.

He viewed the video and listened to his sisters asking Dodge for their own whip bracelets. Heck, if it would keep them safe, he'd buy them one for each wrist.

"Okay, let's get on the road. Personal bikes have been loaded into the covered trailer along with Scoop's vehicle. We'll leave here staggered. No cuts. If they saw your face at the bar, you'll be in the back seat or cab of the vehicles and lying down until we get out of town."

It sounded like a plan to get them out of town had already been worked on while they were rescuing Rose. He trusted his brothers and wanted all of them out and away from that bar and Rose's co-workers.

"Wait, where are we going?" Rose asked.

"We're all heading to the Bluff Creek Brotherhood MC Texas Chapter's compound. We'll figure out what we're doing after we get there, get some food, and make a plan."

"I don't have any clothes," Rose whined.

"What about my job?" Tasha questioned.

"Remington and Beth arrived about an hour ago and went directly to your apartment. They're bringing your stuff. It's not safe for either of you to go back there right now. While they were there, your partner dropped by looking for Tasha." Bootstrap's calm, direct demeanor seemed to be working on calming down the girls, and Scoop was thankful they were listening to him. He couldn't wait for them to be behind the walls of the MC's compound where he could relax a little.

"Hey, how'd they get in?" Rose asked.

"Beth and Remington disguised themselves as a maintenance crew. I believe Beth was Barney and Remington called herself Joe. They told him they were replacing a water heater in your unit. Empty boxes came in and left full. Remi was a little irritated at his attitude. I believe they left a little surprise if your partner tries to take a look-see later. Remi said if and when you go back, they'll disarm it."

Rose stood straighter, walking over to Bootstrap. "If and when? Who do you think you are?"

"Baby girl, I'm the president of the MC who just hauled your ass out of the fire. I say if and when because Cowboy has found some inconsistencies in his research. Your partner may have started with a little prostitution on the side, but he's added in some other not too savory past times. Did you know his last partner's wife and daughter went missing and then his partner was shot and killed on a call?"

Rose shook her head. "I was told he transferred to another city."

"Yeah, to the city of the dead," Dodge remarked.

"For now, I follow what you're saying because it's obvious there's a lot more going on but, I want to make this clear. When, and I say when because it's going to happen, we take my ex-partner and whoever is working with him down, I get a little retribution."

Bootstrap laughed. "You got it, baby girl. If it's in my power, you can pay him back however you want. Load up."

Scoop grasped Sarah's fingers and pulled her toward him. Dropping a kiss on her mouth, he held her in his arms again.

"Did I ever tell you how hot it makes me when you're a badass, fierce woman?"

"Ewww," echoed from his sisters.

He turned to them and rolled his eyes. "Get over it. I'm never going to quit telling her how awesome she is, but let's get on the road."

Chapter Twenty-Two

Sarah leaned back against the chair. By the time they'd all gotten to the clubhouse, it had been dark. They'd unloaded, eaten the meal that had been waiting on them, and then found their rooms. She and Scoop had crawled into bed a little after one a.m. She'd laid her head on his shoulder and had fallen asleep.

This morning, she'd woken up wide-eyed at seven a.m. She'd been anxious to get on her computer. Everything about Rose's situation was bothering her. She'd grabbed a cup of coffee and a cinnamon roll that was on the counter. It hadn't been as good as Regina's, but she'd been starving.

When she'd gone to plug in her computer in the main room, Cowboy had asked if she'd rather use their computer room. She'd commandeered a desk and hooked her computer into their hardline. She'd reviewed what all Cowboy had been working on and then started her own sleuthing. She had a couple searches running and was just waiting for something to come back.

Remi: We're up and in the kitchen. You awake?

Sarah grinned. If she wasn't up and didn't answer them, she didn't put it past Remi or Beth to wake her up. She wasn't sharing any of Scoop's delicious skin with them. She better answer before they broke into her room.

Sarah: Up and running some searches. I'll meet you in the kitchen. I need another cup of coffee.

Beth: I'm hungry so I'm eating this cinnamon roll, but I'm ratting out Gage to Regina that they're serving STORE BOUGHT cinnamon rolls at the clubhouse.

Sarah picked up her cup and headed toward the kitchen. She locked the door on her way out. Cowboy had been clear that the door remained locked even if only brothers were in the clubhouse.

Rose and Tasha were hanging out in the main room as she walked in.

"Have you all had breakfast yet?"

Tasha and Rose shook their heads. "We weren't sure where we're allowed to go."

"Follow me. My sisters are in the kitchen. I need more coffee and maybe another roll."

She pushed open the door. Beth immediately yelled. "So, did you and Rocky Road get some alone time or were you too tired? I was in the room next to you and was waiting for the bed to start hitting the wall, but it was quiet."

Rose and Tasha walking in behind them had Beth giggling.

"Sorry. We have no filter with each other, so you'll just have to deal with hearing about Scoop in bed."

"That's okay. We'll just pretend we're hearing about someone else. Derek's always been so serious and shy. We didn't realize it until later, but he gave up a lot for..."

Tasha interrupted Rose and finished her sentence, "us. We think he deserves someone special and by the look of you and that whip, you're someone special."

"That whip was hawt! I asked Dodge if I could put in an order, and he said we could talk today. I wonder if he could do me a couple in different metals with different looks. Like one with metal stars would have it rip more skin off."

Sarah tried not to laugh at the stunned looks on Tasha and Rose's faces as they just stared at Beth and didn't blink.

"Umm, why would you want more skin ripped off?"

"Tasha, I get you're a nurse, but I'm surveillance and we all do protection jobs. Anything that gives me an edge including something that damages a bad guy enough to allow me extra time to get my client out of there is something I want."

Sarah decided to rescue Tasha. Although Beth's answer was truthful, Sarah was getting the feeling Tasha was a little naïve.

"Ladies, let's get some rolls and something to drink. Do you both drink coffee, or would you prefer something else?"

"Coffee. I couldn't survive a shift at the hospital without coffee."

"Coffee for me too. Is it okay to see if they have any special creamer? After yesterday, I decided calories don't matter today."

At Sarah's nod, Rose had the large industrial stainless-steel restaurant-size refrigerator open. Regina had helped Bootstrap and the other members with the remodel of their kitchen. Both chapters wanted the kitchen big enough to host visiting chapters and large get-togethers.

Shiny glazed concrete countertops stretched the length of the room and covered a large island in the middle. Three large stainless-steel sinks were along one wall with an industrial dishwasher sitting beside them along with a dish drying area. The side of the room closest to the main lounge had a long cabinet with two separate rolling windows that could be opened to pass food through.

Regina had built her dream kitchen because this one was twice the size of hers at the original clubhouse. Unless Baron knocked out the back wall of the clubhouse and expanded, Regina couldn't have this size kitchen.

Sarah could tell Remi had something on her mind. Once the coffee was poured and everyone was digging in, Remi spoke.

"Yesterday, when we picked up your stuff, your partner came by. We brushed him off but set a little surprise for him if he returned. Our motion camera picked up him and two other individuals returning to your apartment and breaking in. Since we were short on time, we had to improvise. It made a little mess, but when he entered, he was drenched in your laundry detergent."

Rose took a second to answer. "Well, if it couldn't be gasoline and a match, at least it was messy. I'm just so angry. I know that he's exploiting kids and women for sure, probably men too. I want to do something."

Beth grinned. "Oh Remi, I think she'd fit in perfectly."

"Fit in perfectly, how?" Rose asked.

"We think your job here is gone because you can't trust your partner. We don't know how high the corruption goes. Obviously high enough to have his last partner's shooting go uninvestigated and tossed in a box. So, we, meaning Franks and Daughters Bail Bonds and our security company, would like to offer you a job. I have something special I'd love to talk to you about once we're back at the compound. You can see if you like it and if not, you could always apply for the sheriff's department. Tasha, I talked to the hospital, and they have an opening if you want on there. It will definitely be slower than the ER you're used to, though. Or the MC is wanting to open a clinic which you'd be perfect for."

Sarah hid a smirk. Remi hadn't paused for a breath, and Sarah knew her sister well enough to know she didn't want the sisters saying no yet. Rose was quiet but she and Tasha exchanged a look.

"I'm good with moving. I only stuck around to keep an eye on Rose. My boss is a total jackass, and I'm ready for a change."

"What the hell, Tasha-Basha. I've only been sticking it out because I thought you liked the hospital. I miss mom and I miss Scoop. Do you think we could convince mom to take a travel job near Bluff Creek for a while?"

Sarah put her hand up before both sisters were off and fighting. By their stance and attitudes, Sarah knew where this was headed.

"Okay, clearly everyone will need to work on sharing their hopes and dreams with each other, but I think it's perfect. I know an offer has already been made to your mom to see if the clinic would be a place she was interested in working. Scoop will have you both around. I'm sure you'll love the MC because we're one big family."

"Woah, you all are leaving?" Gage stood in the doorway. "You haven't even seen all we have to offer. I always have room for help in the brewery."

Sarah kept quiet, but she couldn't see either of Scoop's sisters choosing a brewery over their chosen careers.

"Dude, the scenery is spectacular, but I don't like beer. I'm more of a mixed drink kind of girl," Tasha answered with a wink.

"Yeah, I love Kansas, but Texas is beautiful too."

Sarah laughed along with everyone else.

"Not that kind of scenery, brewmaster. I was talking about the masculine scenery around here. For an old guy, that Bootstrap has it going on." Tasha fanned her face. "When he says baby girl, does it get like fifty degrees hotter to anybody else? No, just me?"

"Glad to hear this old guy has still got it. Though I want to say at fifty-five, I feel like I'm in the prime of my life, not an old guy, baby girl."

Sarah hid her snicker as Bootstrap lowered his voice to growl out baby girl. She was head over heels attracted to Rocky Road, but she had to agree with Tasha, Bootstrap definitely had it going on.

Bootstrap and Gage filled their coffee cups and settled at the table with the girls as Scoop walked in. Her man looked delicious this morning. Tight blue jeans, motorcycle boots, a belt cinching his jeans where his light red t-shirt tucked in underneath his cut. His hair was a tad wet from the shower, and he pushed his glasses up his nose as he walked in.

He walked over to her, bussing her cheek with a kiss on the way to get his coffee.

"I know you have a lot of options. Even though you're welcome here, I don't think it's the safest place for you both right now. The clubhouse in Kansas puts another five hours between you and your old partner's network of criminals. Until we know more about their network and how large it is, no place is completely safe, but the farther away from Dallas you are, the better."

Scoop sat down while nodding at Bootstrap's words. "You know I'd love to have you close, and I agree with the safety issue. The thought that he's only an hour and a half away scares the crap out of me, even with the compound's high walls."

Sarah watched Rose and Tasha communicate without words, just staring at each other. They both turned toward Remi and nodded.

"I want to try working at the bail bonds and security. I need to know I'm making a difference and I'm not ready to trust anyone but family right now. Scoop says you're all family, so when can I move in?"

Tasha giggled with Rose. "Me too. Rose and I have both been saving a lot. I think I'll wait to make a decision on whether I work at the hospital or the clinic until we get there. Do you think since we won't be in an apartment complex, we'll be somewhere we could get a dog or a cat?"

Sarah shook her head. The girls would fit right in with her own sisters and the women who seemed to be joining them. She tilted her head up to look at Scoop's profile.

She was so glad his sister was safe, but she was sorry their trip was ending this way. She wasn't ready to give him up. She didn't know if his words of love were because of the situation or if he really meant it. She wanted it to be real. She wanted to go home and fast forward to them getting married, living together, and having kids. She wanted it all, and she wanted it today. She only hoped he really felt the same way because if not, she wasn't sure what she'd do.

"Animals are always welcome at the compound. My husband and I are picking up our new fur baby in a couple of days. He's at the vet to be neutered and then he can come home."

"Ahh, I can't wait to get a pet. Okay, what's next?" Rose questioned.

Sarah listened to the plans. She'd hoped she and Scoop would at least get to ride back alone to the compound, but it wasn't going to be. The club's tow truck company would be picking up the girls' cars and holding them at a lot until it was deemed safe enough to take them to Kansas or the girls decided to sell them and buy something else. With all the extra vehicles, the girls would have vehicles to drive once they were back in Kansas. She was looking forward to getting to know Rose and Tasha better, but she was honestly petrified to meet Scoop's mom, Stella.

First, she'd never worried about meeting a mother before, but this time, it mattered. Second, where would she and Scoop go next? Fake boyfriend to real boyfriend? She was positive what she wanted, but there had been zero chance to talk about what was next. She was a planner, and the unknown was not something she enjoyed. She'd see what time they were leaving. If they weren't leaving for a few hours, she'd bake a couple items for the clubhouse and relax a little while she was doing it.

Scoop's arm slid around her shoulders, and his fingers played with her hair. She wanted this to be real more than anything.

Chapter Twenty-Three

Scoop had decided he'd had enough. Although he and Sarah had talked and texted this week, he hadn't seen her in person since they'd driven onto the compound. Between helping his sisters get settled and searching for any and all information about Rose's ex-partner, he'd gotten maybe two-three hours of sleep a night.

His sisters had seen Sarah because they'd been over to the bail bonds office, but he hadn't had a chance. He wasn't sure if Sarah was avoiding him or if she'd been as busy as he was. He asked a couple times if they could meet, and she'd had numerous reasons which all sounded plausible. He was worried, and he missed his Firecracker.

He missed lying beside her with her head on his shoulder and her hair trailing down his chest. He missed the smell of her and the feel of her in his arms. And yes, call him a horn dog, but he missed the feel of being inside her and making love to her.

His mom was driving in today. She was expected in a couple hours. and he was going to have Sarah by his side when she did. He also wanted to do all the things they'd missed during their road trip. Her behind him on his motorcycle with her arms wrapped around him. Taking her out for a dinner date without any nervousness about what he'd be learning. Heck, at this point, he just wanted to be in her presence. He wanted to hold her hand.

He pulled his motorcycle into the visitor's parking spot close to the office. He backed his bike in because once he had

Sarah on his motorcycle, he wanted a quick getaway. He wanted a little time with her alone before he introduced her to his mother.

He keyed in the code to get through the gate and walked in the door. He tossed a wave at some of the bail bonds employees. He planned on asking Sarah to leave and go for a short ride where they could talk. If she said no, he'd go to plan B. He only hoped if he employed plan B that none of the bail bonds and security company employees would try to stop him.

He approached Sarah's office quickly and stood quietly in the doorway. She was in a long sleeve V-neck T-shirt and it was tucked into her jeans. She was focused on her computer with one of her suckers stuck in the side of her cheek. No matter how many times he saw her that way, he always got hard. He didn't really want to ride his bike with a hard-on from hell, so he focused on her. She was squinting at the screen and reading. She might be irritated at him pulling her from her work, but he'd given her all the time he was willing to.

"Firecracker, I've missed you."

Sarah jerked and turned toward him in the doorway. Yep, deer in the headlights eyes told him that she had been avoiding him and wasn't prepared to talk about their relationship yet. Well, too bad.

"I've been busy. Now's not a good time."

Scoop shook his head. Plan B it was then. He walked around the desk, cataloguing he wouldn't need to have her change shoes. She had her boots on, not her sandals. He plucked the sucker out of her mouth and tugged her up out of her chair with his other hand.

"What the hell, Scoop," Sarah screeched.

"What the hell is we need to talk. I waited a week, and I can't wait anymore. I need thirty minutes of your time which I don't think is too much to ask."

Sarah's head started shaking. He wasn't accepting no for an answer. He leaned over, placed his shoulder near her stomach, and lifted her over his shoulder. He turned and carried her out the door. Locks was standing in the front office. He smiled at Scoop. When one of the security employees started to get up, Locks motioned him to stay seated. Locks opened and held the door open for Scoop to walk through.

"Daddy!"

"Have fun, Sarah," Locks called.

Scoop hurried through the gate and toward his bike. When Sarah started to say something, Scoop smacked her butt.

"If you want to have our conversation here where everyone can hear it, I'm game. If you'd like some privacy, you'll get on my bike for a short ride over to the racetrack where we can chat alone. Your choice, but make no mistake, we are talking now."

Scoop let Sarah down off his shoulder, making sure she was steady after being upside down. His Firecracker's eyes were blazing and not in the way he loved. Heck, he was surprised she hadn't done some self-defense move on him that would have him lying on the ground in agony.

"Fine."

Scoop got on the bike, waiting for Sarah to take his hand and get on behind him. Once she had her arms wrapped around him, he took off. He wasn't wasting any time getting moving.

SARAH HAD BEEN EMBARRASSED with Scoop tossing her over his shoulder and carrying her out in front of their employees at first. Once they got to the bike, she realized it was kind of hot and he had every right to do something drastic. She had been avoiding him. If they didn't talk, then he couldn't tell her the worst-case scenario she'd dreamed up. Him saying thanks for everything, but I'm moving on.

He stopped the bike at the racetrack she and her sisters had raced dirt bikes on growing up. Once they both got off the bike, he took her hand. She'd missed him so much, but she'd been so freaking scared to talk with him.

Sure, he'd said he'd loved her. But once they weren't together constantly, all her old doubts had crept in. Too old. Too curvy and so many other ones. She'd talked with her sisters, and they'd all told her she was being ridiculous. She wished she could have the confidence they did but she didn't.

Scoop sat down underneath the large tree near the racetrack. He leaned back, opened his legs, and guided her to sit between them. She snuggled back against the man she couldn't live without. If this was goodbye from him, her heart would be broken. Shredded into tiny little pieces that she'd never put back together. Over the last week, she'd realized Scoop wasn't just the man she loved. He was the other half of her heart.

"Okay, I thought it might be easier for you if we aren't looking directly into each other's eyes."

She started to turn around, and he turned her back with her head underneath his chin.

"I have a couple things to say, and then you can talk. Nod if you agree."

Sarah nodded, wondering if this is where he told her they were done.

"I know when we went into this, I agreed that it was a fake relationship, but I lied. I'm not ashamed of it. I was worried if I told you the truth that you'd never consider my request." He dropped a kiss on her head, his hand rubbing against hers. "Sarah, you've been my Firecracker since that first time you called me Rocky Road. You've fascinated me, entranced me until I couldn't even do my job sometimes. Before we ever left on the trip, I knew what end game I wanted. You, in my arms, for the rest of our lives. You are so strong and amazing, yet at the same time, you can be so nurturing. When I envision a future, it's with you. Now, this isn't a proposal. This is a declaration that I want us to be a couple. I want everything with you. I want a house, kids, and whatever else you dream about some day. We had less than two weeks that ended way too soon. I want to give you your fantasy dates and then give you a perfect proposal when you're ready. Now, if I've completely misread the situation and you don't want what I want, then you can rip my heart out. I'll listen and then take you back to your office. I don't know how I'll survive, but I promised you if we did this that we'd still be friends when it was over. I will honor that, though my heart will never be the same because you've stolen a huge piece of it."

Sarah turned. As she placed her finger over Scoop's lips, she stared at the face she wanted to grow old with. His eyes blazed with fear. Fear that she wasn't all in. She was all in. He'd given her everything she'd wished for. She swallowed around the lump in her throat with tears in her eyes.

"You haven't misread the situation. I've always been attracted to you. I lied to myself when I said it was a fake relationship. Every second with you was real, but I fought it. I was too scared to trust you'd want me. I'm older. I have a different body type than all my sisters. I've always had confidence issues, though I fake it to get by. I want the fairytale with you too. And you're not the only one who lost a part of their heart. You're my sexy biker man who rode in and rescued me from a life without love. I want it all with you, including the dates, the motorcycle rides at sunset, and the man who chases bad guys online with me. I'm sorry I avoided you."

Scoop's grin told her all was well with them and then his lips claimed hers. She let the sensations overwhelm her as her sexy biker man showed her exactly how much he loved her.

Chapter Twenty-Four

Scoop dropped his phone in the basket and walked into council. He had searches running and had even had time for a bite to eat before the meeting. When Speedy wasn't annoying him and teasing him about women, he was a pretty cool guy. Slice and Cruise, the men War had invited from the military, had fit right in.

They'd all voted to have their military time count, so their prospect time would be limited to a month getting to know everyone. Scoop knew it wasn't as harsh as a lot of MC's time, but War and Bear had both known them in the military. Serving together counted for a lot.

Scoop took a seat by Flick and across the table from Cannon. As everyone took their seats, Scoop glanced around, wondering where War was.

"Sorry, guys, I had to take him outside one more time. Dog pees more than Rascal, Locks, and Baron put together," War mentioned as he walked in carrying a small dog with a little bowtie on its collar. It was the fluffy little dog that Cannon had laughed about him getting and it definitely didn't look like a guard dog.

"Baron, get your son in order. He's not respecting us," Rascal grunted.

"He's our president and I have no reason to get him in order."

"Thanks, Dad," War smiled at Baron.

"Oh, don't thank me. I'm going to get you back for that remark but not when we're in council. There's a lot of stuff that your mom doesn't know from when you were younger. I might just spill some secrets tonight."

War closed his eyes and shook his head. "I'm never going to one-up you, am I?"

Baron just smiled and put his hands out for the dog. "Let me hold him so you can do your job."

Scoop saw Cannon's eyes light up and just waited for whatever crap might come out of Cannon's mouth about the dog. Before Cannon could say anything, War spoke.

"Thanks, Dad. Luke really seems to like you."

Scoop bit his lip to not laugh at the outrage on Cannon's face. His Firecracker had let him know what Remi and War were doing. Lucas was Cannon's middle name. With them naming the dog Lucas or Luke for short, two dogs were now named after Cannon.

"You know that's my middle name, right?"

War just smiled. "Let's get to business. How's our money?"

Bear pulled out his sheets and slid his readers on. "The diner, garage, tattoo shop, farm, and gun range are doing phenomenal. Bluff Creek Brews had a huge order put in by Nelson's Honkytonk Saloon and Bar. They're giving us a five percent referral fee. Right now, it's in an account waiting for us to decide where it goes. I realize it's the way it's always been done, but doing the books for all the businesses is too much for Regina along with everything else. Plus, she then spends time going over the report with me. As we grow the MC, we've got to take things off her plate."

"All right. Honestly, not only do we need to be adding members, but we need to fill the officer spots that have been left open."

"War, I apologize. When we lost the guys in that accident a couple years ago, I should have had us fill the spots, but they'd been with us so long it was hard."

Scoop had wondered why they didn't have all the officer spots filled and he appreciated Baron owning up that it was on him. As busy as they'd been dealing with issues since he'd came to the MC, Scoop didn't see any way War could have covered everything that needed to be done.

"Baron, it's all good. We'll make a list of what positions we're missing. Then think about who might help out in those areas. Give your suggestions to Bear. We'll meet here in a week after Scoop gives us information on each nomination."

"Uke, Ukey, where are you?" echoed from outside the double doors to the room.

"Uke, we gots treats for you!"

Baron chuckled, "Well, sounds like my grandkids want Luke here to play with. Let me give him to them if that's okay with you, War?"

"Yep, let David and Grant take care of Ukey," War chuckled, looking directly at Cannon.

"I knew you fucking named that dog after me," Cannon yelled.

"Yes, Remi said you'd been a big enough dick that only naming one dog after you wasn't enough."

Cannon glared at War, "And you let her?"

"Cannon, let me be the one to give you this lesson on the Franks sisters. You don't let them do anything. You support them. You love them, but you never tell them you're letting them do anything unless you want your balls to be in your throat."

Scoop, along with everyone else, winced because they all remembered Remi's nutshot to War.

"Anything else?" War questioned, glancing around the room.

"What are we going to do about the girls plastering pictures of us all over the tunnel?" Roam asked.

Scoop wondered if this meeting would ever end. He loved his brothers, but he actually had real problems to deal with like finding the men who were working with his sister's ex-partner.

"Oh, you mean the pictures from the footage you dumbasses forgot to shut off before you streaked? Those pictures?" Locks asked.

"Yes."

"The pictures were up less than thirty minutes. The girls put them up right before you all were sent in to clear the tunnels. And honestly, if you're not smart enough to shut off the video cameras, then you got what you deserved. If you retaliate, don't fuck up any of my stuff. War's prank on Ginger was as far as any of you better go."

Scoop waited to see if their meeting was finally over. He wanted to spend some time with his mom, Sarah, and his sisters. His mom hadn't committed to staying forever, but she was staying for at least six months before she made a decision.

Introducing his woman to his mom had been scary but oh so satisfying. His mom had pulled Sarah into her arms and cried, thanking her for saving Rose. From that moment on, they'd all been fast friends. Regina thought his mom was wonderful and his mom thought the same of Regina. They'd spent a lot of time together over the last week.

He had the girl. He had his family. Now he had to see what was next.

Chapter Twenty-Five

S coop relished Sarah's breasts pressed against his back and her hands wrapped around his stomach. He'd been looking forward to having Sarah snuggled up behind him on his bike. Today was a gorgeous sunny day with only a light breeze. A perfect Kansas day for a motorcycle ride and party with his friends and brothers. They were all participating in the Poker Run. He and Sarah had been the second stop along with Cannon and as the last person came through, they'd all headed out on the route themselves. Speedy as Road Captain had organized the route and been the first spot. Bear and Winnie had been the third stop and had joined them along the way.

They'd wound their way from Bluff Creek to Dodge City, picking up at the stops along the way Hennessy with Kennedy, Ellie and War with Remi. War was leading them, but Scoop's stomach churned as they turned onto the street where Nelson's Honkytonk Saloon and Bar was located. The city had shut down the block with barricades to make room for all the bikes. A couple of large tents were set up because the amount of people was over the capacity of the saloon. Three weeks ago when he'd officially asked Locks for his daughter's hand in marriage, the poker run party had seemed the perfect place to ask Sarah to be his. Now, not so much. He only hoped he didn't disgrace himself.

His mom and sisters had chosen to help man a couple of the booths at their last stop. It had allowed Regina to ride with Baron. Some of their Texas Chapter had come up for the run too. Bluff Creek Brews and the saloon were donating the beer, so they'd be raising more money.

He backed his bike into one of the spaces saved for their club. He held his hand up, steadying Sarah as she got off the bike. He slowly took his helmet off. He didn't know why he was killing time because he wasn't supposed to ask her to marry him until the poker run was over.

His heart was pounding in his chest, and sweat was beading on his forehead. He actually felt a little nauseous, similar to when he puked on her shoes, but today was different. He was stone-cold sober.

Sarah's fingers wrapped around his. "I'm thirsty. I want one of those fresh squeezed lemonades."

He allowed Sarah to lead him over to the tent serving water, tea, lemonade, and soda. Remi was chatting with Winnie. Jesse was close by. She'd chosen to work with his sisters and mom. Beth was taking tickets over where Rascal and Locks were giving trike and motorcycle rides to kids.

He couldn't wait. If he had to wait another thirty minutes, he wasn't sure he'd survive. Her sisters and dad and his mom and sisters were all here. He was asking her now. He got Beth's attention and nodded to her. She tapped Locks on the shoulder. He turned and took a cordless mic from Beth and a box and walked it over to Scoop. Before he handed it to Scoop, he turned it on. Tapping it twice, he yelled, "Yo, quiet!"

The area got as quiet as it could as hundreds of bikers were partying and bikes were still arriving, but the people that mattered from their family were close enough to hear. He took the mic and turned toward Sarah.

He slid down on one knee, holding her hand.

"Sarah, my Firecracker. I honestly didn't think you'd ever even give me a chance after I puked on your shoes." He waited for the laughter to quiet. "You did give me a chance because besides being strong, you are one of the kindest people I have ever met. As I started to fall in love with my Firecracker, I knew I'd have to stay on my toes. You're a smart, badass biker woman who I want for the rest of my life. Sarah, will you be my ol' lady and ride with me for the rest of our lives? And will you allow me the honor of marrying the woman of my dreams?"

He swallowed. Her hand was shaking in his as tears spilled over. She was nodding her head but not saying anything. He handed the mic back to Locks and took his Firecracker in his arms. Sliding his ring on her finger and helping her put the cut proclaiming her as his, had him wiping back tears himself.

He couldn't imagine himself any happier. He leaned down and sealed their fate together with a kiss.

"Mom, Derek isn't sharing his fiancée with his sisters. Will you make him?"

He pulled away from Sarah at his sister's whining. Sarah grinned at him. "You realize we have a lot of sisters to deal with, right?"

"Wouldn't have it any other way, Firecracker."

Chapter Twenty-Six

S arah stood holding onto Locks' arm. Scoop had asked her to marry him, and they'd kicked it into overdrive. An overnight trip to Wichita and she had her fairytale dress. A six-foot train with lace insets, a bateau neckline covered in beads and lace and with Juliet sleeves. When she'd tried it on, she'd known it was the one. Her very own fairytale wedding with her sexy biker man as the prince.

Her flowers shook a little. She didn't know why she was nervous because marrying Rocky Road was everything she wanted. Locks' hand covered hers on his arm.

"Breathe, baby. He's a good man and watching you both, I can tell you have a love like your mama and I did. Heck, he's gotta love you or he would have said no to the monkey suit you have him in."

Sarah grinned. Scoop's eyes had widened when she made her request, but he'd jumped on board immediately. He was in a light gray tuxedo with tails. Her man turned her on in his cut and jeans, but he was swoon worthy in a tuxedo. She could glimpse him through the curtain she was getting ready to walk through. He pushed his glasses up and ran his hand through his hair. She was calmed, knowing he was nervous too.

She'd chosen a traditional gown and a tuxedo for both of them, but she'd picked the song that was special to her. *Meet in the Middle* was the song that was playing in the car when she realized she loved him and wanted him for forever.

Flick and Roam pulled the curtain back as she walked through and headed to her destiny. She wanted to remember every step toward him. She'd known she loved him, but the feeling sweeping through her today was overwhelming. Each step toward who would be the father of her children. The man she'd grow old with.

The kids were all in charge of scattering petals in front of her as she walked. They were doing great, smiling at people as they walked in front of her. She concentrated on them because she wasn't ruining her makeup. No racoon eyes for her on the day she got her fairytale. As they got to the end of the aisle, Phoebe must have said something that angered her brother. David frowned, then dumped his remaining flowers on Phoebe's head.

"Code Ross, Dad," David yelled.

Bear and Winnie each picked up a child and sat them on their laps while Grant calmly skipped over to Roam.

"Sorry everybody," Winnie called out.

Sarah joined the laughter because honestly, she and Scoop had bet there wasn't any way the kids would do everything perfectly. Unfortunately, she owed Scoop twenty bucks because she thought they wouldn't make it even halfway down the short aisle. She'd been positive Phoebe would boss David and Grant which they didn't take kindly to.

"Let's go, baby. Time to marry your man."

Sarah walked with her dad down to Scoop and then Locks placed her hand in Scoop's. Her dad had always supported her in everything. Having him here without her mom was bittersweet, but she'd promised herself she'd focus on the happy parts today. Her dad leaned over and whispered loud enough only she and Scoop could hear.

"Screw this up and you'll be sorry. I'll make sure they never find any evidence."

"I wouldn't expect any less from you. If I screw this up, you have my permission to do whatever. But know this, my Firecracker will burn brighter than she ever has as long as I have breath in my body."

Sarah grinned despite the warning. Her mom had always talked about the type of man Sarah and her sisters would need to find. A man who loved and saw the woman she was. One who lifted her up and helped her achieve her dreams. Despite being younger, Scoop had grown up early. He was the perfect man for her.

Scoop held her hands, waiting on the minister. "Do you think married sex is different?" he questioned.

She couldn't fault his question because their relationship had started out as lessons on how to have sex. She was sure every time would get better. Scoop had definitely caught on quickly, and she was thrilled he had.

SCOOP LED SARAH AWAY from the party, opening the door to the garage. He flicked on a light, locked the door, and led her into the first bay. Her first surprise of the night. Her second was waiting in their house when they got back from a short honeymoon. He'd tracked down the Fiestaware vase she hadn't found on the trip. He planned on continuing the tradition Locks had started with Sarah's mother.

Her second was right here. The smell of motor oil permeated the place, but the garage was pristine. His motorcycle was cleaned and sitting atop a gleaming floor though he'd left a hanger to hang her dress on. Knowing his Firecracker, she'd want to save and preserve her dress for her daughters.

Flick had promised to stand outside the locked door to ensure no one with a key tried to get in. Cannon was doing him a solid and covering the office entrance door. He'd thought through how he could make their wedding night special. He'd come up with the perfect idea when he'd heard Sarah, his sisters, and her sisters talking about one of the books they were reading. They all admitted they'd never had sex on a motorcycle, but it sounded so hot in the books they read. He technically hadn't eavesdropped to get the info. He'd been cycling through the videos of the clubhouse doing a spot check and saw the women talking and laughing. He'd wanted to know why his woman was blushing which she rarely did. Besides the sex on a motorcycle, he knew way more about his brothers' sex lives than he was comfortable with. He'd keep that little secret to himself unless it was needed at a later date.

He'd decided right then that him teaching her something was how he was making their wedding night special. He wasn't sharing, though, that he'd sat on his motorcycle and used a fifty-pound bag of rice to figure out if there were logistics to balancing with the kickstand down and movement on the bike.

He'd decided he'd undress Sarah and himself before they got on the motorcycle. He wasn't going to hurt her because he accidentally dropped her when he was taking her wedding dress off.

"What's this?" Sarah questioned.

Scoop slid his hand through her hair and tilted her up for a kiss. The taste and smell of his woman had him diving in. He could easily lose himself kissing her, but he had a fantasy to fulfill.

"This is me teaching you something tonight." He turned her, slowly unfastening the row of buttons going down the back of her dress. He kissed each inch of skin as he exposed it. Feeling his Firecracker shiver was the best feeling in the world.

"Scoop," she moaned.

He slid the dress off her shoulders, tugging it down past her hips, then bent down. "Hold on to my shoulders, Firecracker, to step out of the dress."

She followed his instructions, waiting on him while he hung up her dress. Sarah was in a corset with her breasts almost spilling out, a tiny G-string, and a garter belt holding up her stockings. Her curvy as fuck figure had him wondering once again if he'd survive to get inside her. Her outfit was completed with the highest fuck me heels he'd ever seen her wear.

"Oh fuck, I have a plan, but you, in that, is making it hard to concentrate."

Scoop swallowed but immediately divested himself of his tuxedo and shoes until he stood hard and ready in front of her. He walked closer until he could wrap his arms around her. Would he ever get tired of the feel of her in his arms? He didn't plan on it. He was going to spend every second showing her how sexy he found her and how much he loved her.

"Wanna fuck you on my bike. How naked do you want to be?"

She trembled in his arms. "Let me slip out of these shoes, but I think you can just slip my G-string to the side. I have wanted you so much today that if you don't hurry, I'll probably come just rubbing against you."

Scoop helped her take off her shoes and got on his bike. His hard dick slapping his stomach. Sarah stood by the bike, and he put his hands on her waist, lifting her to straddle his bike, facing him. He'd been worried about smoothly moving her over onto the bike. He'd accomplished it but now, having her against him, her creamy luscious breasts spilling out of the top of the corset, had him thinking of how fast he could get inside her.

Her heat against him had him wondering if he could hold on long enough to actually get inside her. She'd said she was ready, but what if she wasn't? He wanted her to remember this night and smile. She took his hand down and brushed his fingers against her core. Her pussy was wet, warm, and so ready for him.

"I'm ready. Freaking fuck me, husband."

Scoop smiled, lifted his wife, and smoothly slid into her heat. Without a condom for the first time was better than he imagined. The tight clasp of her walls had him fighting coming, but she was right there with him. He lifted her and slid her up and down a couple times, surging his hips, with her making her sexy sounds, and then she was shaking in his arms. Her tightening on him had him following her over the edge.

He tried to catch his breath and held her to him. His legs and arms had strained a little holding them steady and moving them, but he totally rocked this fucking on a bike thing. He might blush if he ever found out, but his little Firecracker would share her exploits on a bike and put his brothers to shame.

"So, so sexy, my husband. I think married sex is better."

"Me too," he croaked.

"Did you consider clean up without a condom when you were thinking through this set-up?"

Oh fuck. He hadn't. They'd decided once they were married they would quit using condoms. Sarah was quitting her birth control next week. At their ages, they didn't want to waste any time in starting a family. He'd been so focused on how to make love to his wife on a bike that it had never entered his mind, clean up would be an issue.

"Umm, no. How about I try to stay inside you as I get off the bike? If we can reach my shirt, I can clean us up? Or we scoot a little farther back and let it hit the seat."

Sarah grasped his face, pulling him closer. "I love you and love that you made this so special. It was better than any book I've ever read because it was us, my sexy biker man."

Sarah's hard nipples had popped out of the top of her corset and were rubbing his chest. Her lips devouring him had him hardening and ready to go again. He'd worry about how they'd get off the bike later. Right now, he was going to give his Firecracker the wedding night of her dreams.

Chapter Twenty-Seven

J esse listened to the guys whispering. She watched the flashlight beams move around her garage. She'd known there would be payback when she helped steal the footage, but it was oh so worth it. Cannon needed to be taken down a peg or two.

"Come on. Let's do this."

"Cannon, I don't think this is a good idea," Flick whispered.

"Seriously, you are such a pussy," Roam murmured. His flashlight playing over the toolbox against the wall.

"You know, that's really not an accurate term. I mean, I know it's slang, but the pussy is one of the most miraculous things about a woman. It takes a pounding and still does all these wonderful things. When you call me a pussy, you're basically saying I'm awesome." Flick was standing over near Cannon, but she wasn't sure he was actually on board with their prank.

She and her sisters had known the guys would eventually try to pay them back. They'd added a couple of extra sensors that Scoop, who she was sure the guys had checked with, and the other guys didn't know about. If you didn't know about them, then they couldn't be turned off.

"Could we quit the anatomy lesson and get this shit done before they figure out we're here?" Cannon hissed.

Time to let them know their prank wasn't happening. With the items she'd spied them unloading, it appeared they were going to fill her garage with balloons, confetti, and glitter.

The balloons she would have let them get away with. No way was she allowing confetti and glitter all over her garage. There were too many parts that could get screwed up if it got inside them.

Jesse flicked the lights on in the garage and waited by the light switch with her sisters and Ellie and Kennedy. She so would have included Scoop's sisters if they hadn't been busy.

"Too late. What exactly did you think you morons were going to do in my garage?"

"Pay you back for your prank," Cannon retorted.

"I'm confused. You're acting like we did something to you. As far as I know, you did something to yourselves. You went streaking outside without the cameras turned off. All we did was get a copy of the video." Beth high-fived Jesse as she finished.

"And have pictures made and hung in the tunnel," Roam bitched.

"Oh, the big bad biker man didn't want his dick hanging on a wall. I mean, if you didn't want everyone to see your dick, then why did you take your clothes off?"

Roam glared at Ellie but didn't reply to her.

"I'm completely fine if you want to fill my garage with balloons. Tomorrow, I'll even scream oh no, who did this to me, but there will be no glitter or confetti. It could hurt the engine parts or the weapons I have in here. I'm a little disappointed that you didn't think of that Cannon, or maybe you just don't care."

Flick rolled his eyes and shook his head. "I mentioned that to everyone, but did anyone listen? No, it was Flick, you're a baby. Are we an MC or are we pussies? I finally gave in because Roam wouldn't shut up."

Jesse couldn't hold it in once her sisters were all laughing at Flick.

"Fine, let's leave. This isn't over and I will be getting you all back!" Cannon shouted.

"Sure," Jesse pushed the button, raising her side garage door. She motioned to them. "See yourselves out."

The guys grabbed their stuff and walked out the large garage door together. Beth pressed a button and buckets of cold grape Kool-Aid doused the guys as they left.

"Now, you have something to pay us back for!" Beth yelled.

Jesse looked around at her sisters and the women who'd joined their little group and knew they'd always have her back. She was incredibly lucky to have such an amazing support network. At some point, she was going to need to let them in on her little secret. But for now, until she knew how she was going to handle it, she'd keep it to herself.

Chapter Twenty-Eight

Sarah snuggled into Scoop's side as she listened to everyone talking. Sunday lunch was the one time they all tried to be together. As they added more people and family, getting everyone together was hard. Stella, Rose, and Tasha had fit right in. Tasha and Rose had taken over Remi's house since Remi and War were in their new one. Stella was staying in a room at Locks' house until she decided exactly where she wanted to be. The clinic was up and running despite a couple of hiccups.

The daycare for their family was running well. Sarah was pleased with the people they'd chosen to allow close to their family and take care of their most precious people.

It had been three months since Scoop's puking on her shoes and she couldn't be happier. Things had changed so much since the guys had come back to Bluff Creek. Bear and Winnie were almost at the six-month mark of the kids being with them. War and Remi were settled in to married life. If they could get their demon dog, Luke, to quit doing so many naughty things, then it might be calm for a little while.

She had her man, her family, and hopefully sometime in the next year, she and Scoop would start a family. She'd thrown out her birth control the week after they'd tied the knot and they'd started trying. Watching Winnie with the kids had made her ache even more for a baby. One with Scoop's hair and eyes. Sappy, but she loved sappy. Scoop was her hero on a steel machine. It hadn't happened yet, but she was hopeful. If not, she and Scoop had discussed there were so many children in the world who needed someone, and they had room in their hearts. Only time would tell but Sarah was happy. She and Rocky Road were debating whether they were staying in her house close to the bail bonds office or building close to Remi and War. It was a hard decision, and they were taking their time.

Jesse was scooting farther away from Cannon, who was beside her. They seemed like oil and water. Cannon definitely had the domineering vibe going on. Jesse was strong, fierce, and not willing to listen to any crap. Locks had started Jesse in the garage when she was nine, learning about anything mechanical. Sarah still remembered the black eye Jesse gave a boy after he called her mean names because she liked cars. It would take a special man to understand Jesse.

Jesse avoided Cannon any chance she had. How they ended up by each other at lunch was a mystery.

At some point, if she didn't quit moving, she was going to end up in Slice's lap. Slice was one of the ex-military guys who came to the MC while she and Scoop were on their trip. She'd been ready for this badass name about how he sliced up his enemies. She and her sisters had almost rolled on the floor because they were laughing so hard when they learned about his name. He was named Slice because he always asked for an extra slice of bread at mealtime. He owned it, talking about a growing man needed his fuel. Regina always had an extra roll or slice of bread for him. He was bulky with muscles stretching his T-shirt. He definitely didn't look like he ate too many carbs.

"Woah, sweetie," Slice reached to catch Jesse as her chair started to tilt. To keep her from falling, he grabbed her around the waist. His eyes bulged as his hands cupped Jesse's stomach. Jesse sat up straight and was looking down at her lap.

Cannon growled, "What the fuck" and reached over, pressing his hand to the bulge under Jesse's overalls she'd taken to wearing everywhere.

"Are you fucking pregnant?"

"That's a swear, and it's a secret, shh," Phoebe whispered.

"Yep, a surprise and 'prizes can't be talked bout," Grant nodded his head.

"We keep the 'prize and we get a special present, right?" David smiled and high-fived Grant.

Jesse looked at the kids. "You guys did a great job and yes, you kept the prize. Since the cat's out of the bag, I'll share. I'm pregnant. I'll be welcoming my baby in about three and a half months."

"Whose baby is it?" Cannon barked.

"It's my baby, not that it's any of your business." Jesse stood up to scoot her chair back. Slice held her elbow as she got up.

"Get your fucking hands off her," Cannon snapped.

Sarah wasn't sure how to help her sister, but she spotted her dad walking around the table. When Cannon went to grab Jesse's arm, Locks stopped his hand from touching her.

"Cannon, I like you. You're a brother, and that means something, but we always treat women with respect and if you don't want me to teach you a lesson, you'll change your tone."

Cannon shoved his hand against Locks' arm, moving him out of the way.

"Is it mine? Are you carrying my baby?"

Jesse turned back toward Cannon. Sarah wanted to know as much as Cannon did. Jesse had never let out a peep about

Cannon. Sarah had been so wrapped up in everything going on in her own life, she realized she hadn't been there for one of her little sisters. She was correcting that right now. She got up and walked over to where Jesse was standing.

"Do you want me to give you a ride home, or would you rather come to my house?" Sarah slid her arm around Jesse for support, waiting for her answer.

"I want to go to your house if it's okay," Jesse whispered.

"Jesse, you'll have to answer me sometime. Is it mine?"

Sarah could feel Jesse trembling in her arms. Remington, Winnie, and Beth had walked around the table and were waiting to go with her and Jesse. Her sisters always took care of each other.

"Like I said, the baby is mine." Jesse turned and Sarah led her out to the car.

Chapter Twenty-Nine

Scoop got the text that it was okay to come home and had immediately hopped on his bike. Today had not gone like he'd thought. He had the new tattoo he'd gotten. He'd planned on a late afternoon ride, then showing her his tattoo.

After Sarah had left with her sister, he'd texted her to say he'd stay at the clubhouse until it was okay to come home. He'd even offered to stay at the clubhouse if Jesse wanted to spend the night and didn't want him there.

It was getting dark by the time he'd gotten the all-clear. He pulled his bike into the garage and went in the door to the kitchen. Sarah was standing, sipping a cup of hot tea with red eyes. He immediately kissed her forehead, pulling her into his arms, and she set her cup down.

"Are you okay?"

"I am. I'm fluctuating between kicking his ass or helping him win my sister. I'm not sure which will win out."

Scoop brushed a kiss against Sarah's forehead. "Can I do anything right now to help?"

Her arms tightened around his waist. "You're doing it. You're always here for me. I want my sisters to have what I have. It's Jesse's story to tell, so I can't share much, but I will tell you, my sister's heart is broken. I only hope it can be mended."

He lifted Sarah in his arms and carried her toward their bedroom. If he couldn't help her sister, then he was going to cheer up his woman. He walked into their bedroom, putting one knee on the bed as he laid his Firecracker down on it.

"Got a surprise for you," he said, taking his cut off and hanging it on the hook for it. He pulled his T-shirt off with his back to Sarah. He turned and walked toward the bed. She sat up higher in bed when she saw his chest.

By the time he was at the bed, she'd moved to her knees and was reaching for the wrapping protecting his tattoo. Her smile spread across her face as she read his tattoo. He'd had Roam design one that read Firecracker's Biker Man.

"I love it," Sarah whispered, kissing his neck.

"I wanted everyone to know I'm yours too. Now, what do you say we celebrate my new tattoo by me worshipping every inch of your body?"

Sarah leaned closer to kiss him but paused as both their phones went off.

Scoop grabbed his phone, handing Sarah hers.

"Code Ross. Something's happened to Cannon."

Scoop caught the shirt Sarah tossed at him. Cannon had been at the clubhouse when he left. He'd been sitting talking to Speedy and Flick. He'd calmed down from earlier and had agreed to not contact Jesse until the next day. Flick had been asking the guys if they wanted to go on a night ride and they'd been considering it when he left. He only hoped his brother was going to be okay. Whatever happened, Cannon wouldn't be alone.

Scoop held the door to his Bronco open and buckled Sarah's belt before brushing her lips with a kiss.

"Do we need to see if Jesse wants to go with us or wait until we know more?"

The End

Thank you so much for reading Scoop and Sarah's love story. If you loved it, please consider leaving a rating or a review. Ratings and reviews are how you can help other people find The Bluff Creek Brotherhood MC.

If you want to get glimpse of what happened with Jesse and Cannon, you can grab a bonus scene here: https://dl.bookfunnel.com/t0zrmtz03u

The best way to stay in touch is in my reader group or my newsletter. If you want to chat books, join my reader group Steamy Swoony Romance Reads. We have a book club each month and chats.